Y0-BDG-259

BARBARA J. LANGNER

The Detectives Who Loved Opera

Copyright © 2013 Mysterious Valley Press
Cover design by: Robin McClannahan
All rights reserved.

ISBN: 1484169042
ISBN-13: 9781484169049

I

"The chandelier rocked back and forth several times before it crashed into the empty seats below. The sound of breaking glass and splintering wood thundered throughout the theater. It was awful! Luckily the entire opera cast was rehearsing on stage. We all stared in horror at the fragments of glass and smashed seats. Dust and debris flew everywhere," said Hugh Atkins, the artistic director of the opera.

Monica listened to his story and shuddered as the two of them drank coffee in the teachers' lounge. "It's just like *The Phantom of the Opera* here in Albuquerque."

"Yes, I thought of that, too." said Hugh.

"I'm glad no one was under the chandelier," Monica said. "Do you know why it fell?"

"They're investigating, but it appears the wire was frayed, and the metal link weakened from age. The Kimo is an old theater." Hugh pushed back his long, black hair from his eyes.

"It's still odd that it broke." Monica wrinkled her forehead. She loved the old theater with its distinctive Native American decorations. The brightly painted murals depicted nineteenth century pictures of Native American towns called the Seven Cities of Cibola. Small lighting fixtures shaped like cow skulls gave the theater a rather exotic appearance.

Monica's slender hand held her cup in the air while she contemplated this freak disaster. "The maintenance men should have noticed the frayed wire and weakened chain," she said.

"Most people don't look up at the ceiling for defects. And by the way, the falling of the chandelier wasn't the only unusual event although it was, by far, the most chilling."

"What other things happened?" asked Monica.

"Last week a blood-red stain appeared on a chair. Two days ago we smelled a foul odor in the dressing room. Later, we found a dead black cat in the trash. On a lighter note, sandwiches, leftover pizza, and even salads have mysteriously disappeared from our little fridge for weeks."

"No one admitted doing any of those things?"

"Every single person denied responsibility. After the chandelier crashed, two women in the chorus panicked and quit on the spot. I'll have to replace them quickly. Monica, would you help me out and join the chorus?" Hugh looked nervous and drained of all energy. He removed his glasses and rubbed his eyes.

Monica really wanted to help Hugh, who taught choral music at Four Hills High as his day job. "I'm in my church choir, but I'm not a great singer. But if you're desperate for a soprano, I'll help you out."

"Thanks, Monica. I really appreciate it. Do you know anyone who sings alto?"

"Leslie does. She used to sing in a trio. I can ask her since she's my best friend."

Hugh removed his glasses again and polished them with his handkerchief. He put them back on and blinked a couple times. "I have another favor to ask you."

"What is it?" Monica took a sip of coffee and waited for his answer.

"You're good at figuring out mysteries. Would you be willing to investigate the theater's problems? There's a lot of talk about this phantom. Some hint he wants to destroy the production or even go as far as harm a cast member. The only way to stop all this talk is to catch the prankster who's been doing these things."

"Sure, I'd be happy to investigate. Miss Marple, Jessica Fletcher, or Stephanie Plum would never turn down a request to delve into a mystery."

Hugh chuckled. "You've told me before about your fascination with detective fiction so I thought you might be interested."

"In my secret daydream life, I imagine myself to be like one of my super sleuth heroines." Monica smiled and set down her cup. "I'll be happy to try to solve Albuquerque's case of the phantom of the opera."

After leaving the lounge, Monica went directly to her room to do prep work for teaching English 12. While she thought about the crashing chandelier, she wrote the rules for semicolon usage on the board. She could hardly wait until passing period so she could talk Leslie into joining the cast of the opera.

When the passing period bell rang, Monica bolted out the door almost as fast as the kids. She met Leslie in the hall between their two classrooms. They both leaned against the wall and watched one boy trip on his dangling shoe laces and another jerk his jeans down so low his pants sagged at a dangerous level. Nothing unusual.

"I just spoke to Hugh who told me about the chandelier plummeting down into the seating area at the theater during a rehearsal of *Carmen*. He needs to replace a couple singers in the chorus who got scared and left," said Monica as she ran her fingers though her short, brown hair. She had on a tweed blazer, crisp white blouse, and high heels. According to her theory on teacher clothes, a jacket gave her clout for keeping order.

"I bet those people got jumpy because of the show, *The Phantom of the Opera,*" said Leslie who took a bite from an apple, her break snack. "It was an eerie, spooky show."

Monica looked at her watch. The short passing period was almost over, and both women had to return to their classrooms. "I agreed to fill in for the soprano, but Hugh needs another alto in the chorus. Would you be willing to sing?"

"I don't know. I always thought operas were dull although I've never seen one. I just remember seeing cartoons about the opera. Usually old men in the audience snored while a fat soprano wearing a horned helmet and carrying a spear bellowed out a high C." Leslie munched a little faster on her apple after she, too, peeked at her watch.

"In this production of *Carmen,* both the star soprano and mezzo-soprano are thin, and they don't wear helmets with horns. It's a great music spectacle. You'll be humming some of the popular tunes as you leave the rehearsal. It's fun being in a show," said Monica hoping to persuade her friend to join the cast.

The two of them often spent time together to collaborate on lesson plans, pass judgment on the new principal, attend the school's basketball games, or sip a cappuccino on a Saturday morning at the Flying Star restaurant.

Leslie said, "I like Hugh. He's doing a great job with the chorus here at the high school, and I'd like to help him out." Leslie paused and added, "But rehearsing at night and teaching during the day won't be easy."

"I know, but we're young. We haven't hit 30 yet. We can grade our papers while we're not on stage since the chorus doesn't sing much." Monica subtly implied only old people concerned themselves with activities at night while holding down a day job.

Because of her constant flow of energy, Monica was able to handle evening events while still preparing lessons for teenage minds. She planned an enactment of Act III of *Henry V* for tomorrow's class. She had plastic swords that the boys always used with great swashbuckling gusto during the battle scenes.

"Okay, okay, I'll do it. I might regret it later, but I'd like to help Hugh out."

When the bell rang, the conversation ended since they had classes to teach. Both women were smart, attractive, and liberal, but their styles differed. Monica wore suits, sweater sets, and heels while Leslie liked long dresses, floppy tops, and Birkenstock shoes. During the last year, each purchased a hybrid car, a Toyota Prius, to cut down on pollution.

That night when Monica and Leslie entered the theater for rehearsal, they heard Belinda, the star of the opera, screaming at Hugh. "I can't sing with all that noise. Tell the prop men to quit dragging furniture across the floor. It grates on my nerves."

Belinda's lips tightened into a straight line as she stalked off the stage in a snit. Her deep auburn hair, worn long and straight, bounced as she walked. The other singers looked at the director to see how he would handle the situation.

Hugh trudged over to the pouting diva, put his arm around her shoulders, and purred, "Sweetheart, I'll talk to them. I'm sure they can work on the scenery at another time. You sang your aria beautifully tonight."

"My nerves are so delicate," said Belinda as she sat down on a folding chair near the cast's snack table. She crossed her long legs and inhaled deeply.

"You'll be fine in a few minutes. I'll get you a cup of tea." Hugh poured hot water over a tea bag in a cup and handed it to her. He shouted at the cast, "Take ten."

Monica and Leslie wandered over to a group of singers lounging on folding chairs during their brief recess. Most of the chatter consisted of comments about Belinda's behavior.

One of the women said, "It's not the Met, for God's sake. She's acting like she's a prima dona, like Maria Callas. This is a local show in Albuquerque with a volunteer cast and orchestra."

Others made similar remarks.

"Who does she think she is?"

"We'll never get out of here if Hugh has to baby her every night."

Leslie whispered to Monica, "I've heard she's a pain in the ass all the time and not just when she's singing the lead in an opera. The men don't seem to mind probably because she's gorgeous and has a big chest. Did you notice she unbuttoned her blouse practically to her navel?"

Monica added, "And it's a size too small."

Meredith Grainger, who sings the soprano role of Micaela, sidled over to Monica. "I hope you won't get discouraged with all the problems the company is having. The chandelier crash put everyone's nerves on edge, especially Belinda's. In general, she's a difficult person, but I'm sure things will work out."

Monica agreed with her friend. "You're right. I've heard a bumpy beginning means a smooth ending. Besides, no phantom haunts the theater. Old worn-out metal caused the chandelier incident, and some teenage joker probably enjoys pulling the other pranks and scaring the adults."

Hugh returned on stage and signaled with his hand the rehearsal would resume. The orchestra members picked up their instruments, the singers ambled on stage, and Belinda waited in the wings for her cue.

"We're supposed to smoke cigarettes, but we'll be using candy ones," whispered Monica to Leslie. Maybe I didn't tell you, but Hugh wants to make this production cutting edge so instead of nineteenth century Spain, we're in Rome, B.C. Instead of a cigarette factory, we work in a cottage industry making Jesus Christ Sandals. JC is the brand name."

"But if the opera takes place B.C., how could we already have the Jesus Christ brand name?" asked Leslie.

"Hugh says no one will notice," answered Monica with a shrug of her shoulders. "It doesn't bother me, and in opera you have to suspend your disbelief anyway."

Monica and Leslie walked on stage with the other chorus girls, pretended to hold a cigarette, and sang about the soothing pleasures of smoking. The song ends with the pessimistic view that the words of love are nothing but smoke. Monica loved this foreshadowing of the conclusion of the opera.

Belinda as Carmen, the impudent gypsy girl, strutted on the stage. She flipped her long hair, let her eyelashes flutter, and sang the popular "Habanera." In the song, love is a willful, wild bird which can't be tamed. Monica observed that Carmen's flirtatious glances at the soldiers along with her sinuous hip twists and wiggling breasts wove an erotic spell.

Milt Grainger, in the Don Jose role now changed to Joseimus, appeared to be enchanted with the gypsy girl. After catching the red rose Carmen had tossed him, he put it in his mouth and clenched it with his teeth. He did a little jig, removed the soggy rose, and pressed the flower to his chest. A lock of his blond hair flopped down over his forehead which he smoothed back quickly.

After the end of Act I, Belinda became sulky again. "Hugh, I want the tempo faster. But I can't rehearse any more tonight. My voice needs rest. I mustn't tire my voice."

After complaining to Hugh, Belinda walked over to Milt and pulled him aside. She said to him under her breath, "I don't like your bizarre reaction to my rose." The two continued talking in the wings.

Monica turned to Meredith and asked, "How does your husband like singing with her?"

Meredith sighed. "He can't stand her. Every night he comes home and grouses about all the dustups she caused."

"How do you like singing in the opera?"

"I love my part as Micaela, changed to Flavia. I have a couple of great arias as the country girl who loves Joseimus."

Suddenly with a loud kerplunk, a paint can dropped off a shelf and spilled paint on the backstage floor. The entire cast jumped on hearing the noise.

Belinda yelped, "My nerves! I can't take it." She sat down at the table, poured another cup of hot tea, and stroked her throat with her hand.

"It was just a paint can," said Hugh as he sat down beside her.

One of the prop men picked up the can and wiped up the drops of spilled paint. The singers and orchestra members waited in place while Hugh soothed Belinda.

After he spoke a few words to her, he addressed the company, "That's all we'll rehearse tonight, folks, but the costume mistress wants to take measurements. The chorus girls and the soldiers will wear white Roman style costumes which will provide a background for Carmen's brilliant red dress."

The tenor, Milt Grainger, spoke in his rich, vibrant voice, "I feel Don Jose, or rather the Centurion Joseimus, should wear a color that stands out. Perhaps a brilliant blue tunic." Milt stood feet apart as he often did when he sang.

"Red, white, and blue? Don't those colors seem a little out of place in Rome, B.C.?" needled Hugh with a trace of sarcasm in his voice.

"A red dress doesn't exactly fit either," responded Milt dryly.

Hugh stroked his chin. "How about a brown tunic?"

"I feel, as the male lead, I should stand out in a bright color. Besides, I look hideous in brown." His barrel chest heaved, and his handsome chin jutted out.

Hugh raked his fingers through his hair while he tried to cajole the tenor. "You look good in brown, Milt. You really do."

"I will *not* wear brown!" huffed Milt who took a deep breath and expanded his chest several inches. To Monica, he looked like a bird that had just puffed out its feathers.

"How about a royal purple?" suggested Hugh. "You look great in purple. We'll find a deep shade that will blend with your eyes." Monica noticed the fluttering of a tic in Hugh's left eye. It reminded her of the police chief's spasm when he met with Inspector Clouseau in that series of movies.

Milt considered this color suggestion for a moment and said, "Fine, but I want to select the exact shade." He strode off the stage and went over to talk with Belinda.

Monica and Leslie lined up for measurements. "If we're wearing togas, the costume mistress doesn't need to be overly concerned with sizes. I suppose length matters, but otherwise togas are pretty full and floppy," commented Monica while yawning. "I'm ready to go home and hit the sack."

From offstage, Monica could hear Belinda and Milt talking. "Milt, I insist you don't stuff my rose in your mouth and do that funny little tap dance. Just clasp it to your heart as any sane man would do after a beautiful woman tosses him a flower as a sign of affection," said Belinda.

"Darling, I am showing the world I am thrilled with this flower a beautiful woman has tossed to the handsome man who has caught her eye. It's a gesture celebrating the moment. I am dancing, pardon the cliche, with joy. Afterwards, I'll clasp the bloom to my heart." After explaining his point of view, he put a pencil in his mouth to represent the rose and pranced around as he clicked his heels.

"You look like Snoopy doing the flamenco with a bone in your mouth," argued Belinda in a strident voice while she sucked in her breath and tapped her boot on the floor. "Freakish behavior should *not* be part of an opera."

"It's not freakish. Joseimus is a man elated with his rose, and his dance steps aren't odd. Those steps are his celebration of life. You, on the other hand, flounce around like a low class stripper."

Belinda's eyes hardened, and just as she was about to reply, Hugh intervened with calming words. "Everyone's nerves are a little on edge tonight. I'm sure neither of you meant what you said. Let's just get a good night's sleep, and we'll all feel better tomorrow." The two combatants strutted off in opposite directions with their noses in the air.

Hugh's tic scrunched up not only his eye but the muscle in his cheek.

Later, as Monica and Leslie were putting on their jackets, they saw Hugh sipping coffee and watching the prop men nailing some boards together for the tavern scene in Act II. Monica walked over to him, patted him on the shoulder, and said, "You have quite a job. I'd heard about ego clashes in opera productions, and now I've seen it. Whatever are you going to do about the rose and jig controversy?"

Hugh shrugged his shoulders. "I'll try to figure out a way to keep them both happy. Frankly, the rose in the teeth reminded me of a comic tango dancer."

Monica thought for a moment and suggested, "Perhaps he could smell the flower and clasp it to his chest. Do you think he would go for that little change?"

Hugh grinned. "Who knows? I thought working with adults would be easier than with kids. Right now, I'd like to be directing my teenage students."

"I understand. See you at school tomorrow," said Monica heading for the door.

As she approached the short flight of stairs that led to the outside door, she tripped, fell to one knee, but managed to stay upright. She had stumbled over a small box in the middle of the floor directly in front of the steps. As she rubbed her knee, she groaned, "That box wasn't here earlier."

Leslie, who had been walking with her, bent down and helped her up. "I agree the passageway was clear before. Why is it here?"

Other members of the company gathered around Monica who was dusting herself off. They all stared at her.

"The phantom of the opera did it. He's right here in this theater," proclaimed a woman from the chorus. Monica thought that she spoke with such positive assurance as if she herself were a messenger from the spirit world. The comment caused some tittering from the group.

Another person chimed in, "It could be the ghost of the man who was murdered in the theater six months ago. I don't remember his name, but a man was stabbed to death here on the stage. They found his body in the morning. He was lying right there in a pool of blood." She pointed to a center spot on the stage floor, and everyone's eyes followed her finger. "They had to replace the boards because the blood wouldn't come out," she solemnly added.

No one laughed. Monica piped up, "Why would a ghost want to move a box?"

The messenger of the dire news said, "He doesn't want anyone to disturb him."

"There have been lots of plays produced on this stage before this opera," retorted Monica, who was a little disgusted no one argued or laughed at this outrageous story.

Milt Grainger broke into the group with chilling words. "That man was my brother. I have difficulty talking about his death, but his spirit would never hurt a production. He was an actor himself. He loved the stage, and he died on the stage."

Milt paused as he pulled himself together. "No one knows who killed him. I doubt if we'll ever find out. I don't want to hear anything more about Rob or his ghost."

The company became very quiet. Voices mumbled various apologies.

"Sorry, we didn't know."

"So sorry about your brother."

"I'm sure he's not responsible for the mishaps."

Milt charged out the door followed by his wife. After hearing the door slam, the woman who had stated with certainty the phantom of the opera was responsible for all the incidents, walked over to the spot and proclaimed in a solemn voice, "Evil will return."

The company members stared at her. Two people crossed themselves, another tittered, four of the musicians guffawed, but most remained speechless for a few seconds until the nervous laughter caught on, and everyone started to chuckle.

Monica whispered in Hugh's ear, "Who is the bad news messenger?"

"Cassandra Keller. I really don't know her very well. You know how superstitious some people can be."

Monica whispered back, "Cassandra in Greek mythology had the gift of prophecy, but no one believed her. Odd isn't it that she just predicted a grim future, and everyone is laughing."

As Monica drove home, she thought about all the happenings of the evening. She loved to read mysteries and wanted to write one herself. Perhaps she could use this setting.

She definitely would call Albuquerque Police Detective Rick Miller, her almost boyfriend, and tell him about the unusual events at the theater. Maybe he could give her some information about the death of Rob Grainger.

2

On the following night, Monica and Leslie arrived at the theater a little early. When Monica entered through the stage door, she greeted the elderly guard, "Hi, Pops." She thought calling the old man Pops echoed all the old Broadway shows she had seen in the movies. Leslie rolled her eyes and poked Monica in the ribs.

Monica heard a cacophony of sounds: the voice of Belinda doing a warm-up exercise, the violins running through the first aria, and the tapping of the tympani by the drummer who was tuning his instrument. Off to the side, Milt was practicing his "celebration of life" steps with a wilted rose dangling from his mouth. After thinking about the rose and jig, which sounded like a British pub, Monica had a plan for at least part of the problem.

Monica walked over to Hugh and said, "I have an idea to end the rose in the mouth."

"Sure, try it. I agree with Belinda. It's out of place."

Monica sauntered over to Milt, cupped her hand over her lips as if she were giving him a secret message and murmured, "I heard the chlorophyl in the stem will stain teeth." Immediately he dropped his jaw, and the rose fell from his mouth.

"I never heard that before. Can you see any green stain?" Milt opened his mouth and used his fingers to pull back his lips from his teeth.

Monica leaned in and scrunched up her eyes as she examined the enamel. "No, they're just fine. You were lucky," she said in her serious voice.

Milt fished around in his pocket, lifted up a small mirror, ran his tongue over his front teeth, and inspected them closely. "You were right. No stains. My God, that was a close call." Milt sat down and sighed with relief.

While most of the cast members wore jeans and tee shirts for rehearsals, Milt wore Dockers and an ironed white shirt with the sleeves rolled up and the first two buttons open. He looked trim and clean-cut. No stain would dare appear on his person Monica thought.

Hugh, the director, called out, "Act I, cigarette girls, Joseimus, and Carmen."

Monica pulled out the candy cigarette she kept in her jeans pocket and took her place on stage. Leslie carried hers as she followed Monica. As they all sang their parts, Monica wondered how the rose and jig would go.

Carmen tossed the flower to Joseimus who caught it and placed it over his heart and not in his mouth. No dance steps followed. Evidently the "celebration of life" had gone away. Belinda, as Carmen, turned her sexy twisting and wiggling down a couple notches. To Monica, it appeared compromise had been achieved.

Tonight Meredith, called Flavia instead of Micaela to fit the Roman theme, sang her soprano aria about her love for Joseimus and about his mother's love and hope that he should return back home to the little village. Monica thought a man's conflict between the good girl and the bad girl kept reappearing throughout the centuries.

In this opera production, Monica noted the singers represented the roles they played. Meredith, a home body, cleaned and cooked for her husband and children.

She attended church every Sunday and baked cup cakes for PTA fund raisers.

On the other hand, Belinda wasn't bad, but she flirted with men constantly. She touched them on the shoulders, fed their male egos with compliments on their muscular arms, and often gave them the "bedroom" eye by dropping her eye lids while speaking to them. She had been married three times, never cooked, and wore sexy clothes.

The two women, however, competed in vocal performance. They criticized severely the daily renditions of each other's singing.

During a break, Monica overheard Belinda talking to Meredith. "Darling, you were marvelous, but you were a little flat on that high A."

Meredith lifted an eyebrow and cooly answered, "But I, at least, didn't miss any of my entrances. You were a beat off and had to rush your first eighth note to get back on tempo, dear." Both women smiled in a sickly sweet manner and sauntered off in opposite directions.

After overhearing these little digs, Monica walked over to the coffee pot and found Leslie munching a doughnut. "I hope all goes well tonight," commented Monica. "Hugh is already a nervous wreck."

"I've heard we're going to do all of the first act which includes the fight offstage and the pretend scuffle when Joseimus is supposed to take Carmen to jail but instead lets her go free. I'm eager to see how well the lead singers can act," said Leslie.

The chorus rested while the act played out. From within the sandal factory came screams, thumps, and yells. The victorious Carmen, looking like she had been having tea with the Queen, sauntered out the factory door.

Hugh walked over to her and said, "Sweetheart, you need to pretend you're a wild gypsy who's just had a hair pulling, knockdown fight with one of the girls. You look too good, too perfect."

Belinda lifted a lock on the side of her hair and pushed it towards her face, pulled down her peasant blouse until it barely covered one of her breasts, and gathered her skirt to expose more leg. "Is that better?"

Hugh paused and said, "We'll work on that a little later. Let's continue with the dialogue. Joseimus, you must look bewitched with this beautiful woman so the audience is convinced you will go against the order of your superior and let the gypsy escape."

After Belinda and Milt took their places, the music began. Belinda, as Carmen, coquettishly charmed Milt, the innocent centurion. When Belinda arched her shoulder against his chest, Milt did a little twist so he stood in front of her. She moved in front of him while singing seductively. He sang his response and stretched out his arm in a huge gesture which completely covered her face. Quickly, she ducked under his arm and stood directly in front of him as she sang.

Monica wanted to giggle but knew she didn't dare. She merely cupped her hand over her mouth like she was hiding a yawn.

When Milt, as Joseimus, allowed the enchanting gypsy to escape, she skipped off stage while he extended both arms in a grand finale gesture.

Hugh said, "That was great, but we need to work on the blocking a little more." His tic appeared again as he spoke. "That's all for tonight, folks. Tomorrow we'll do the tavern scene."

The cast members picked up jackets, threw away paper cups, and trudged towards the stage door.

Suddenly Belinda ran across the stage screaming, "This isn't funny. Who did this?" In her hand, she was holding a black paper rose. "I found this on my dressing table. Well, who did it?"

"Darling, don't look at me," responded Milt.

Cassandra, the previous bad news bearer, narrowed her eyes and hissed, "The ghost did it. It's a warning." Cassandra's eyes focused in an intense gaze on Belinda.

"Oh, for God's sake, someone just played a little joke on you. The more you react, the more he'll keep it up. There are no ghosts," Milt declared. He grabbed his wife's arm and walked off the stage.

Although Monica heard snickering, she noticed a couple frightened faces. Maybe Hugh was right, and someone was trying to subtly sabotage this production. But why?

Belinda dropped the black rose like a hot potato. "Why would the ghost send me a black flower? He doesn't even know me," she wailed.

"The dead have knowledge of many things. If you really want to know what's happening, you need to seek someone who can get you in contact with them," advised Cassandra in a low voice. " Llorona speaks to the spirits."

Monica interrupted, "Around here, everyone calls her *La* Llorona, and she's just a myth, not a real person."

Cassandra said, "I don't know why she doesn't use the *La*. I've never asked her, but she's a real person who lives in a little house on the edge of town in the South Valley."

"According to the story, she's looking for her dead children," Belinda said as her eyes grew wider. "As a kid, I was scared of her. We all were."

Cassandra spoke again, "This Llorona gives seances and talks with the dead. Also, she gazes into a crystal square and gives you information about your future."

"Whoever heard of a fortune-teller who uses a square. You mean a crystal ball, don't you?" asked Monica who furrowed her brow in puzzlement.

"No, it's a crystal square, a cube. She looks into it and sees all sorts of messages and people from the spirit world. Crystal balls are definitely out, old-fashioned, not twenty-first century at all. Mediums, seers, fortune-tellers use new technology." Cassandra instructed not only Monica, the skeptic, but also the other members of the company who had stayed to hear about unworldly things.

Belinda stared at Cassandra. "Carmen reads the tarot cards and sees death in her future. And I'm Carmen. Do you think there's any connection?" stammered Belinda.

Monica noted the change in the lead singer. From being the haughty diva, she now appeared to be a scared child.

Feeling common sense must prevail, Monica said, "Of course not. Tarot cards can't tell the future. Neither can crystal balls or squares or triangles. This Llorona person tries to build a mystique to attract customers. She's a fake, just like all fortune-tellers."

"There have always been disbelievers," said Cassandra smugly. She sniffed, turned away from the group, and headed for the stage door.

Everyone in the company started to talk at once. Some shrugged their shoulders, others laughed, and a couple made the sign of the cross.

Belinda tapped on Monica's arm and pleaded, "Would you take me to see this Llorona person? I don't want to go with Cassandra. I want to go with a skeptic."

Monica didn't answer immediately, but she gathered her wits together and said in a soothing voice, "I think you'd just be throwing away your good money. Why do you want to go?"

"Carmen believes, and when I sing those beautiful songs, I feel I am Carmen. When we do the scene with the cards, I'm afraid I'll see death, too," blurted out Belinda who almost broke out in tears.

Hugh had overheard this ghost talk but wasn't concerned until he saw his lead singer get freaked out. He put his arm around her shoulders and purred, "Darling, the opera isn't real life. Nothing is going to hurt you. Would you like a cup of tea?"

"No tea. I want to see Llorona. Monica, if you don't go with me, I'll go alone," declared Belinda in a strong voice.

Hugh quickly looked at Monica and pleaded, "Go with her. Please go with her."

"Well, I don't know," stammered Monica. She looked at Hugh whose left eye scrunched up in a big tic. "Okay, I'll look up her phone number, and we'll go," conceded Monica who really liked Hugh and didn't want his nerves to get worse if she failed to appease the show's star.

"Thank you so much," gushed Belinda. "Please tell me tomorrow night when we can see her and get a reading or seance or whatever."

"Okay, I'll run down the information and tell you tomorrow night at rehearsal," promised Monica.

On the way home, she asked Leslie, "Will you go with me? It'll be an interesting experience. I'll drive."

"No, I don't want to see some crazy, old woman with a crystal square. It probably is an old aquarium she's adapted in order to be a twenty-first century seer. What a waste of time," grumbled Leslie.

"I thought in the fortune-telling business the seers didn't care about the new technology. Cassandra acted like we all should know they did. It would be kind of funny if she used a cell phone, a computer, or an iPhone to contact the dead. I'm intrigued by this Llorona person." Monica tossed out her thoughts as she drove.

"You can tell me all about it afterwards," said Leslie as she stifled a yawn.

As Monica stopped in front of Leslie's apartment, she added, "I'm doing this visit to this so-called clairvoyant to help Hugh, but I think it'll be kind of fun."

After Leslie jumped out of the car, Monica headed for home. She anticipated a visit from Rick who said he would pop over for a minute after he finished some paper work at the station.

She had only been home for a few minutes when Rick knocked. He used the rhythmic pattern of shave-and-a hair-cut-six-bits. Mitsey, Monica's rescue dog from the pound, barked in happy little yips since she recognized the pattern. The dog, a lab mixture with black fur and white spots over her eyes, ran to the door as she always did when she heard that familiar noise.

Monica greeted him with a little kiss, and Mitsey did the same when the tall, lanky man leaned down to pet her black, furry head. "Ah, kisses from my two favorite girls," he commented.

"Which one is your real favorite?" teased Monica as she grabbed his hand and walked him into the living room.

Rick furrowed his brow. "I'll have to think that over. Each of you has endearing qualities," he bantered.

Mitsey followed him so closely her nose rubbed against his pant leg. After he sat down, he petted the pooch some more.

Rick pushed back a lock of black hair that had fallen over his forehead. Since he was off duty as a detective with the Albuquerque Police Department, he wore jeans and a sweat shirt.

"How was your rehearsal? Any strange happenings?" asked Rick.

"Belinda became hysterical when she found a black paper rose on her dressing table. Cassandra suggested she see a seer named Llorona who lives in the South Valley, and I'm going with her," said Monica as she went into the kitchen to make coffee. "Have you ever heard of such a person?"

While she was in the kitchen, Monica quickly ran a comb through her short brown hair and put on more lip gloss.

"No, I've just heard about the Llorona legend. But you know how these psychics like to come up with odd names."

Monica's two cats strolled out of the bedroom, saw Rick, leaped on the sofa, and plopped themselves into his lap. He stopped petting Mitsey and switched to the kitties, Marilyn and Bob. Mitsey behaved herself and acted like she didn't give a yip. "How has your day been?" Rick asked as he stroked their soft fur.

"You have completely won over all my animals," said Monica as she set a cup of coffee on the table for him. Monica admired all of Rick's good qualities: his intelligence, integrity, kindness, and love of animals. Also, she valued his opinions. "Tell me, what do you think about my visiting this seer person?"

"You're throwing away your money, but I imagine you know that," said Rick.

"Hugh is so desperate he told me he'd pay for it. Belinda sings beautifully, but she's so emotional. I think he's afraid she'll quit," added Monica as she took a sip of coffee.

"By the way, we arrested several fortune-tellers during the state fair. They picked the pockets of their clients and may have given them a sedative in tea or some other drink," Rick cautioned.

"Don't worry. I won't drink anything, and I'll watch my purse. I think the experience will be fun. My curiosity has been aroused about how she rigs her crystal square."

"Crystal square? I've never heard of that before." As he laughed, he jiggled the cats. Annoyed by the movement, Marilyn hopped onto the top of the sofa while orange Bob stayed on his lap. Mitsey nudged Rick's leg with her nose to get more attention. Rick sipped his coffee and gave Mitsey another pat before he switched his eyes to Monica who had more to say.

They enjoyed talking about even the small daily events. Monica was blown away by the fact Rick, a detective, read Shakespeare's plays and attended opera performances. She, on the other hand, liked to hear about police investigations and wanted to be an amateur sleuth like Miss Marple, Jessica Fletcher, and Stephanie Plum.

After he left, she remembered she had planned to ask him what he knew about the stabbing death of Robert Grainger on the stage of the Kimo Theater. She wanted to get more information so she could solve both mysteries: the theater prankster and the theater murderer. Tomorrow she'd search for clues.

3

"Good morning, am I speaking to Llorona?" asked Monica who scrunched the phone between her right ear and her shoulder.

"Yes, I'm Llorona." The voice sounded weary. "I don't look for lost pets. I won't scare children who behave badly or who are on drugs. I am a medium. I can contact the spirits and answer questions about the future or the past." She sounded like she had repeated that introduction a zillion times. "Now, can I help you?"

"Yes, perhaps, you can help me. I have a friend who sings the lead in the opera production of *Carmen*. In the opera, Carmen sees death in the tarot cards, and my friend who's singing the role fears it could apply to her. Could you give her a bright future? Something indicating she'll sing beautifully in the opera, and you might even go so far as to say she'll become famous. Could you do that?" Monica blatantly said what she wanted.

"The crystal square never lies," responded Llorona.

"But could you?"

"Well, my dear, you don't beat around the bush. My readings are $25. If you want a rosy future, that's $15 extra," negotiated Llorona. "If I see a tragic future, I will override it with my skill. Perhaps I'll see instead just what you want. I can't tell, of course, until I look in my crystal square."

"Why do you use a crystal square?" Monica just blurted out the question. "Ever since Cassandra told me about crystal squares, I've been intrigued."

"Darling, there's less distortion in the square. I can see the dear departed much clearer, and I don't have to bend my head to read the written messages. A curved surface leads to the possibility of misinterpretations. A flat surface is really a much better medium, if I may make a little joke." Llorona chuckled.

Monica felt negotiations were going very well. "I'm glad you're pleased with your new device. Getting back to my friend, could you give her a really, really good future. For example, could you say you see her singing at La Scala or at the Met? She would be tickled pink."

"You do want a glowing future for her. If you say she has the voice for it, I could mention the Met for perhaps an extra $10. I don't want to stifle vocal talent. I used to sing myself, but it interfered with my business."

"I'll pay the extra money. It would give her so much happiness to believe she's going to sing in an important opera house."

"Is there anyone in the Other World you wish to contact? I'll give you a discount since you're bringing a paying customer," offered Llorona.

Monica pondered the latest offer. "I have an aunt who passed away four years ago. She left me her pearl necklace which I can't find. It was a beautiful necklace, and I'd like to wear it. Do you do lost and found items?"

"Usually, I don't. Often the departed have changed their minds about their stuff. But I'll try it. The discounted price is $20."

Monica had one last question. "Why do you use the name Llorona and leave out the *La*? She's called La

Llorona around here, and she isn't an oracle in the local myth. She just weeps at night and looks for her dead children. Everyone is frightened of her."

"I hate *La*. It makes me think of 'Deck the hall with boughs of holly, fa, la, la, la, la etc.' All those *las*. Dreadful. But I like the name recognition of Llorona. Madame Arcati, Madame this or that are names people around here think are brothel owners. Llorona has mystique, scary reverence, and believability. The name might not work in Chicago," conceded Llorona.

"I look forward to meeting you. Could we come on Friday night? We rehearse Mondays through Thursdays. By the way, I should have told you before my name is Monica Walters, and the singer's name is Belinda Bridgers," explained Monica as she concluded the business.

"Friday night is fine. I'll see you then."

Elated about the availability of a good fortune, Monica no longer felt nervous about taking the impressionable Belinda to the fake, but agreeable, Llorona. She knew Hugh would be very pleased and might spring for the cost. Keeping the star happy was a top priority in an opera production.

On Friday night, Monica picked up Belinda for their date with the psychic. Both Monica and Belinda dressed casually in jeans and sweaters. As they wound their way through the old, curvy streets in the Valley area of the city, Belinda stammered out her fear, "Maybe we shouldn't go. What if she confirms what Carmen saw in the tarot cards?"

"Remember Carmen is just a fictitious character in an opera by Bizet," soothed Monica. "The composer just wanted to make the opera exciting."

After getting lost several times, finally Monica found the house at the edge of the populated area of the city. Several blocks separated each house since this area previously had been inhabited by people who farmed. No trees, a few mesquite bushes, weeds, and empty space would provide a perfect setting for the landing of a space ship from Mars.

The gravel crunched as Monica parked in the driveway. A light went on, and a woman dressed in a long blue gown with a black cape appeared on the porch. "Hello, did you have trouble finding my little house?"

Belinda didn't move a muscle. Monica poked her head out of the car window and politely lied, "No trouble at all." She gave Belinda a little nudge and whispered, "She looks like a nice, old lady. Let's go."

As they walked to the door, Llorona gazed at them with an intense scrutiny. She faced Monica and declared, "You're Monica. I can see from your face you're a person with great thoughts." She switched to Belinda, "And you, my dear, have the face and bearing of a distinguished singer." After swirling her cape, she turned and gestured for them to follow her.

Llorona didn't wear a turban or a scarf over her head, but instead let her silvery hair hang down over her shoulders. Every now and then as she lead the way, she flipped her hair back while the black cape floated behind her. To Monica, she resembled a female Merlyn from King Arthur's court

Monica discreetly asked, "What is your opinion about genies in bottles? I remember a TV show where a genie could grant wishes. Do you do that?" Monica felt a little naughty about asking these questions from a fake, but she was curious how she would answer.

"Don't mention that dreadful TV show to me. It's a disgrace for all of us oracles. There are no genies in bottles or in lamps. Someone made up the story that genies pop out of bottles. I know what comes out of a bottle, good old hooch. Also, we soothsayers don't grant wishes. We speak to the dead or use other secret methods of finding out what will happen in the future."

Monica wanted to ask Llorona her opinion on Harry Potter's training in a special school, but Llorona trudged ahead out of earshot and opened the door to her living room.

The darkened room, lit only by five candles, revealed shelves of books in disarray, vases with dead flowers, a stuffed ferret, lots of little bottles with stoppers, and a computer. A brown sofa and two lumpy chairs faced an open fireplace that warmed the room with its golden fire. On the coffee table in front of the sofa sat a large cube covered with a striped, fringed scarf.

Llorona guided them into the room and said, "Please sit on the sofa. It's so cozy to face the fire, don't you think?" Both women sat down as told.

"Would you like a cup of tea? I have my own special brew."

Remembering Rick's story about the pocket picking fortune-tellers who might have given their clients a drug, Monica declined the tea for both of them. "Thank you, but we're not thirsty."

"Very well, let's begin. I'll scoot the table over a little more so my crystal square is in front of me," said the oracle as she sat in one of the lumpy side chairs. She whipped off the scarf like a chef who's presenting an award winning gourmet concoction. The crystal square gleamed on the table with an eerie light.

"Isn't she beautiful?" bragged Llorona as she stroked the sides of the luminous square. "Besides my square, I need my cat. She's my familiar."

"Do you work with both a crystal square and a cat?" Monica asked. "I hadn't heard of that combination before."

"My cat likes to work with crystal. Some familiars won't have a thing to do with crystal, but my Pyewacket uses it. She has other means of contacting those who are in the Other World, too," explained the seer. At that point a black cat jumped on the table, peered into the square, and pawed at one of its sides.

"Pyewacket, my darling," crooned Llorona as she stroked the fur on the black cat. "I named her Pyewacket after the cat in the old movie, *Bell, Book, and Candle.*"

"I think it's a lovely name," said Monica. "I have two cats, Marilyn and Bob. Marilyn is mostly black with a big white patch on her back, and Bob is orange."

Llorona removed her cape and got down to business. "Belinda, please ask your question."

"I want to know my future," croaked Belinda whose eyes darted around the room in a frantic fashion.

"Place your hand on the square. Spread your fingers so your aura can pass through," instructed Llorona.

Belinda's shaky hand rose slowly and landed on the top of the square.

"Now, we wait," Llorona said softly. Under her breath she chanted in Latin, swayed back and forth in an undulating manner, and closed her eyes.

Soon the crystal square had a storm of white particles like a snow toy turned upside down and shaken.

The little flakes moved around and finally settled. Small fish appeared; one looked a little like Nemo to Monica.

The black cat showed a great deal of interest in all the particle activity and pawed the top of the square. Belinda kept her hand in place while her eyes widened. Monica surreptitiously peeked under Llorona's chair for evidence of electronic machinery. She looked on the wall and the ceiling for wires or switches, but she couldn't find any.

A pleasant smell of apples and cinnamon wafted in the air. Monica wondered if the fortune-teller had just baked an apple pie. Apple pie, a good American symbol, didn't fit in with seances, spirits, or mumbo jumbo.

Snowy particles still floated in the crystal while Llorona chanted a spell in Latin. The black cat meowed several times while she pawed on the glass, but nothing else happened. Monica became a little restless, uncrossed her legs, and looked at a stapler dangling from the paws of a stuffed ferret in the cluttered room. Belinda didn't move a muscle but sat stiffly.

Suddenly in the middle of the square, Monica saw tiny notes of the first two measures of the "Habanera," Carmen's famous song. Monica and Belinda's eyes opened wider when tiny hands appeared and started clapping. Belinda started to hyperventilate as the crystal revealed three letters, MET, followed by more clapping hands.

The show ended with a wild snow storm in the crystal. Once the snow settled, the cat jumped down, and Llorona shook off her hypnotic state.

"My dear, I saw a wonderful future for you. You will be very successful in your current endeavor, and in fact you will even sing at the Met. The spirit has spoken. Did you see the signs in the crystal?" asked Llorona with a flourishing gesture at the square.

"Yes, I did, I did. I can't believe it. The Met! Everyone tells me my voice is wonderful, but now I know I will go far." Belinda bubbled over with enthusiasm and excitement. In a dramatic gesture, she reached over and grabbed Llorona's hand. "Oh, thank you, thank you."

Monica hugged Belinda who was still in a dither. "It's wonderful. You're going to sing at the Met," said Monica while she strained her eyes looking for the projector or whatever device Llorona used.

"My dear, do you have a question for the spirit?" asked the seer who faced Monica.

"It's not as important as Belinda's. In fact, it's so trivial I hate to mention it, but my aunt left me a pearl necklace. I can't find it," said Monica.

"I'm not a lost and found source. But since the spirit is giving off such strong energy tonight, I'll try. The spirit has good nights and bad nights, and tonight the vibrations almost knocked me over. Perhaps she'll help you. How many strands were in the necklace?"

"Two strands," answered Monica who wondered why she wanted to know.

"Pyewacket jumped on the table again, but instead of clawing at the glass, she sat on top of it and licked a paw. "She's not interested, I'm afraid," commented the seer.

Suddenly the cat leaped on top of Monica's lap, looked at her, and meowed four or five times. "My dear, you are in luck. Pyewacket just said your male cat knows where the necklace is. Ask him when you get home."

Monica didn't know what to say to this foolishness. Taught to be polite, she said, "Thank you. I'll check with Bob when I get home. Bob is my cat," she explained. She scratched Pyewacket behind her ears while she purred in contentment. After a few minutes, the cat jumped down and stalked out of the room.

Llorona smiled as she said, "Bob will show you where the necklace is."

Monica looked at the beaming Belinda who handed the seer a $50 dollar bill. Evidently splendid news generated a big tip. Monica added the money Hugh had given her and another twenty for her pearl necklace advice.

Since Monica taught *Oedipus Rex*, she had to ask a literary question. "Have you read about Teiresias, the blind seer?"

"Of course, my dear. Sophocles thought he was so clever by creating a blind seer, an oxymoron everyone can recognize. You don't have to be blind to be a seer. You need The Gift, which is rare. I was born with it, but through training I have expanded my abilities."

"How did you train? I just finished reading all the Harry Potter books, and I wondered if you went to a school or something like it," Monica added lamely. Since she believed all fortune-tellers were phonies, she knew Llorona would be making up her background, but she wanted to hear the quack's cover story.

"I trained with a spirit named Nancy who entered the Other World as a young woman with her cat. Animals often go to the same place as their owners. She sent a cat to me and said she would be my connection to the dead, the residents in the Other World. I named her Pyewacket although Nancy thought the name pretentious. She liked Lulu better."

"Pyewacket is a lovely name. She must be a very smart cat." Monica felt good manners dictated that a visitor should compliment the hostess on something.

"Yes, she is, but I beat her at chess most of the time."

"Your cat plays chess?" Monica's voice reflected her incredulity.

"Of course, but usually I win. She tends to make the same moves over and over so I can anticipate what she plans to do. She doesn't like to sacrifice her pawns, even if it helps get her queen in a better position. I hate to say this, but she's a sore loser. Last night she knocked all the pieces off the board after I won for the third time."

"I'm still impressed."

Belinda didn't show any interest in Pyewacket's abilities or Llorona's credentials. Monica suspected Belinda's desire to believe her good fortune overrode any technicalities.

Belinda hummed a few bars of an aria. She stopped short and spoke to Llorona. "Could you come to the theater and talk with the spirit of a man who was murdered on stage? He might be the one doing some odd pranks in the theater. You are so talented. It would be wonderful for the entire company to know what has been going on."

"A man was murdered on the stage? When did it happen?" inquired the seer.

"About six months ago, Rob Grainger, Milt Grainger's brother, was stabbed on the stage of the Kimo Theater. Since we've had strange occurrences there, I wonder if his spirit has been trying to contact us. Could you come down and talk to him?"

"How intriguing. I don't know if Pyewacket would want to make the trip. She doesn't like to ride in cars. She gets car sick. But I'll walk around the spot and use my own methods to speak with the spirit."

Belinda had a suggestion. "You could ask Rob's ghost if he'd like some special food or drink. We could leave a bottle of Crown Royal on the table in the Green Room. His brother told us that was his favorite whiskey." Belinda evidently thought after a couple shots, the ghost wouldn't be interested in black roses or leftover pizza in the fridge."

"Usually the spirits aren't interested in spirits, if I may make a little joke. But I've known a ghost who used to be roaring drunk when I contacted him. It was rather embarrassing when I had to tell his loved ones that Daddy was still hitting the bottle in the Other World. He had been sneaking booze out of their liquor cabinet at night." Llorona shook her head as she remembered the antics of the tipsy ghost.

Belinda continued her plea for Llorona's intercession. "Maybe he wants his killer punished. If he gives you the name, I'm sure the police would be glad to put the murderer in prison. Then Rob might feel better and leave the opera production alone."

"I'll go. The cost is $100 because it sounds like a complex situation," mused the fortune-teller.

"Oh, I'm sure Hugh, our director, would be happy to pay you $100," chirped Belinda. "I'll tell him how marvelous you are."

Monica thought if Llorona had predicted a bad future for Belinda, she wouldn't be so marvelous.

"I'll come on a night when there is no rehearsal so the spirit can hear my incantation clearly and won't be distracted with lots of people milling about," said Llorona.

"Since this Friday night the theater is dark, you'll have a perfect quiet time for summoning the ghost. I'll get Hugh to open the stage door. Monica and I will be there, too," said Belinda.

Monica didn't care she had been roped into this additional seance since her curiosity about Llorona's methods kept nagging her.

She thought she knew how the seer had rigged the reading for Belinda even though she hadn't seen any machinery. She figured some sort of overhead projector had been aimed at the square. Probably the notes, the clapping hands, and the letters MET had been projected by Llorona flipping a switch or else an accomplice running the machine in a back room. How would she manage on an open stage?

"Very well, I'll come this Friday at 8:00," said Llorona who ended the conversation with a nod. She escorted the two women to the door and waved after they climbed into the car.

All the way home, Belinda glowed and babbled about her golden future. Every now and then she'd run through an arpeggio.

At one point the two gossiped about the members of the company. Belinda murmured, "I think the chorus girls should know Milt has a roving eye. His poor wife doesn't have a clue about his philandering. Don't worry about Burt. He's gay."

Monica perked up. "Milt is a skirt chaser?"

"Yes, darling, he's a tenor. They all are. I know. I was married to three of them. They all sang beautifully, we blended our voices in duets, but, alas, they were unfaithful," Belinda sighed as she spoke of the wicked ways of tenors worldwide.

"I'll warn Leslie." Monica had a lot to tell her best friend which included the seductive tendencies of Milt, one of the tribe of deceitful tenors. As soon as she dropped Belinda at her house, she'd call Leslie and tell all.

4

The next night when Belinda entered the stage door for rehearsal, she announced in a loud voice, "I'm destined to sing at the Met. That wonderful seer revealed my future."

Meredith pooh-poohed her news, "Darling, an old woman with a cat isn't really worthy to evaluate your voice. There are music critics, you know, who are trained to find talent."

Most of the chorus members yawned and went about their business.

Monica started to feel a little guilty. She whispered to her friend, "Maybe I went too far with the Met thing. Perhaps I should have just told Llorona to indicate Belinda's success with this opera, which I think will happen. Now Belinda really believes she's going to be a superstar."

Monica chewed her lower lip as she considered her overzealous request to the fortune-teller. Nervously, she hiked up the sleeves of her blue cardigan sweater.

"Don't be a worrywart, Monica. Belinda probably thought she was headed for the Met before she even saw Llorona."

"And another thing, Belinda wants Llorona to come to the theater and conger up the spirit of the murdered man for $100. I don't want to push Hugh into spending more of his money."

"It's up to Hugh to decide about investing $100 to placate his lead singer. It's not your decision," consoled Leslie.

"That's true. If he does spend the money to keep her content, maybe it's worth it. We all want the show to be successful." Monica tried to justify her meddling.

"A little mumbo jumbo can't do any harm," Leslie added.

"It could. Bringing in Llorona to talk to the dead Rob might unnerve the company more since it'll draw attention to this so-called ghost. Too bad Cassandra keeps saying freaky things," moaned Monica.

Their conversation was cut short as Hugh announced they would begin with the scene in the tavern. The stage hands had constructed a saloon bar with high stools and a sign that said "Lillimus Pastimus." In keeping with the Roman theme, they had added several couches with only one side raised. To Monica, they looked like psychiatrists' couches ready for a group analysis.

Hugh told the women's chorus to use huge leaves to fan the centurions who drank their wine while reclining. Monica and Leslie picked up the palm leaves and slowly waved them back and forth to get the feel of the gesture.

After Hugh had blocked everyone's position, he signaled for Act II to begin. The musicians played, the gypsies danced, the girls waved their leaves, and Carmen sang.

The raucous arrival of the toreador, now Spartacus the gladiator, heightened the excitement of the scene, and the entire cast became electrified with the music and storyline. As Belinda tossed her hair, twirled in a flirtatious way, and sang her lines, Burt, as

Spartacus, responded in an equally seductive manner with his gorgeous baritone voice.

The magic of the moment ended when Burt leaned his arm on the bar to pick up his glass of wine. The bar suddenly fell over with a thunderous crash when one of the legs split and another buckled and shattered. Caught off balance, Burt teetered for a moment but managed to stay upright.

"What the hell?" he shouted. The music stopped, and the cast stared at the collapsed wooden bar.

"It's the ghost," hissed Cassandra.

"Faulty carpentry," whispered Monica to Leslie as she brought down her arm which was getting a bit fatigued from the constant swinging up and down with the palm leaf.

Belinda clasped her hands together and moaned, "I hope I don't get another black flower. Hugh, you must get Llorona to talk to the ghost. She'll fix it."

"Oh, for God's sake, Belinda, do you really believe Rob's ghost just broke a tavern bar? That's crazy," blurted out Milt.

Hugh checked out the broken bar. "I can't tell what happened, but I'm sure no spiritual being destroyed this piece of furniture."

"My nerves. I can't sing when I'm nervous. I have a delicate nature," squeaked Belinda in a little girl voice.

"I could have fallen over and broken something," whined Burt who cracked his knuckles evidently as a nervous gesture. "I heard of another singer who fell and broke his leg. After being set, the leg became infected, and the germs traveled through his blood stream and into his throat. He lost his voice. Couldn't even make a squeaky sound. He never sang again."

No one paid any attention to his dire predictions of the consequences of breaking a limb.

Burt continued, "I could have injured my voice if I had fallen over and landed on my neck." He ran through a couple arpeggios to make sure he could still sing.

Monica wondered how anyone could land on his neck after tripping over a piece of broken furniture.

Meredith, who had walked back to her dressing room just before the furniture disaster struck, returned holding an artificial black rose. "Look what I got," she announced.

When Belinda saw the flower, she lost her nervousness and became rather indignant. "You got a black flower? Are you sure it wasn't for me? I got the first one, so I certainly am the one who is supposed to get the black flowers. After all I am the star."

"My part as Flavia is very important. I am a true soprano, not a mezzo-soprano," retorted Meredith. "I can hit a high C." After Meredith asserted her superiority, she tossed her black flower in the closest trash bin.

"A high C means nothing. It's the quality of the voice that matters," huffed Belinda.

Monica looked at Leslie, rolled her eyes, and whispered, "Keeping Belinda happy is quite a job. I hope Hugh is up to the task."

The focus of the cast had slipped from Burt to the squabbling women, Belinda and Meredith.

Monica noticed Burt tried to regain attention to himself. He stood and moaned again about possible injuries. "I could have twisted or broken my ankle. How would I be able to sing if I was on crutches?" No one answered this rhetorical question.

Milt broke in, "Let's get back to rehearsing. Forget the broken bar. Let's start the scene with the smugglers, right before my entrance."

"I don't know if I can sing. My nerves are shattered. I feel faint," whined Belinda.

Hugh put his arm around her. "Darling, I know this is difficult, but you are a real trooper. I know you have star quality inside that will make you strong." He cajoled, "Let's give it a try."

Belinda inhaled deeply and nodded. "Hugh, dear, you are so right. I'll try."

Burt snorted around and acted like he begrudged this return to the opera. Monica and the cast members, bored with the moans and groans of the stars, happily took their places. The orchestra members geared up, the prop men picked up the pieces of broken wood, and the rehearsal continued.

After Hugh ended the night's practice, Monica searched out Joe, the set designer, and his assistant, Nick. "What's your take on all these pranks?" she asked the two men who had pieces of the broken tavern bar in their hands.

Joe, the bigger and brawnier of the two, said, "Look at the place where the leg was nailed to the side. It's been sawed. I finished this piece of furniture last night, put it on the back of the stage, and left about 11:00. When I arrived about 6:00 p.m. this evening, it was in the same spot. I didn't check it out. Why should I do that? When Hugh wanted to set up for Act II, I just moved it."

"I've never heard of a ghost who used a saw, have you?" chuckled Monica.

Both men laughed. "That dame really got upset with all that talk about spooks. Believe me, the joker has two legs and a strong arm. Some people get their kicks in strange ways," he added.

"Who has keys to the theater?" asked Monica.

"I don't know. I have a key along with Pops and Hugh. The theater manager does, of course. Probably anyone could have one made. There's a spare key hanging in the supply room." Joe stroked his chin while he thought.

"It seems to me this prankster has some knowledge of the theater which would mean he or she has performed on the stage before or is a member of the opera company. But if you're a member of the company, you wouldn't want to sabotage the show." Monica paused for a moment and then asked the two men, "Who would have a motive?"

They shook their heads. Monica lowered her voice, glanced around, and said, "Would you like to find out who this scalawag is? All you would have to do is arrive at odd hours. Instead of 6:00, come at 5:00 or stay later. Maybe you could catch someone dropping off a black rose or moving an object."

"We could do that," affirmed Joe, "but I'm not going to sit in the dark for hours like they do in a police stakeout."

"No, I wouldn't expect you to do that." Monica realized it would be impossible to know when the prankster might come. "Just keep your eyes open for any clues," she said.

As Monica and Leslie were leaving, Hugh came over to them. "I promised Belinda I would hire Llorona. I know it's like throwing a $100 bill down the toilet, but she keeps after me. She says she's nervous and might faint."

"She does seem to like attention," drawled Monica. "Frankly, I think someone should just tell Belinda to suck it up."

"I'd rather pay the old seer lady than tell Belinda to suck it up." Hugh shuddered at the thought of the repercussions that could follow such a suggestion.

"Well, yes. Belinda might be upset. If you like, I'll come along for the seance or whatever. Llorona told me her cat doesn't like car rides, but she can still reach the spirits by herself. Maybe if you give her a bonus, she'll say whatever you want her to say. She'll have to put on a show and go through some sort of hocus-pocus first, of course."

"What do you mean?" asked Hugh.

Monica couldn't control her strong desire to spill the beans so she said, "She charged more when I asked her to tell Belinda she would sing at the Met."

Hugh whooped at the news and convulsed so hard he got hiccups. After he finally calmed down, he croaked, "I love you, Monica."

Monica said, "Maybe if you give her an extra $50, she'll say there is no ghost, and the prankster is a teen-ager who wants to scare the dickens out of the adults. Do you think that would calm Belinda down?"

"I hope so. Well, good night. I'm glad the evening ended with a good laugh,"said Hugh as he opened the stage door for Monica and Leslie. All three of them chuckled as they thought about the mercenary seer.

When Monica returned home, she rang up Rick and told him about the events of the evening. "Some-one sawed through the leg of the wooden saloon bar so we know the other events weren't just carelessness on the part of the crew. The black roses have a sinister aspect. I think some prankster wants to sabotage the production. Could the police do anything?"

"You can file a report, but ordering a stakeout because a couple women got black roses and a wooden bar was broken won't happen. You, my dear Miss Marple, will have to figure it out." Rick enjoyed needling her about her interests in detection.

"I'll try, but so far I haven't a clue. But I've alerted the prop men to be on the lookout for a stranger with a key. Tomorrow night I'll be curious to see how Llorona works without her crystal square or cat. Do you want to watch?"

"I'd like to come, but perhaps I'd spoil the evening."

Monica said, "Why?"

"If she knew I was a police officer, she might not appear. Taking money under these circumstances is a little iffy although it's small potatoes. Some of these scam artists can swindle people out of thousands of dollars," Rick said.

Monica answered, "I thought that's what you'd say. How about homemade cherry pie with vanilla ice cream here at my place after the seance or whatever she calls it?"

"I'd like that in a big way. When should I come?" he asked.

"I don't think she can put on a one-woman show for longer than 30 minutes. I'll call you when I leave the theater," promised Monica.

After they hung up, Monica remembered she needed to buy some cherries. She wanted to bake a super good pie to impress Rick with her domestic ability. The date with Rick was more important than the mumbo jumbo of an old lady, but her curiosity had been aroused. What would Llorona do?

5

Monica, Hugh, and Belinda waited on the stage for Llorona exactly at 8:00 on Friday night. Belinda nervously paced back and forth while Monica and Hugh talked about school events. Monica guessed people who dealt with the occult probably didn't care about worldly things like watches while she and all her fellow teachers lived by the clock.

At 8:30 the stage door opened. Llorona whooshed in with her long skirt whirling around her legs, and her black cape flying behind her. She carried an enormous tote which she put down by her feet. "Good evening," she croaked in a foggy voice.

"Good evening," they replied in unison.

"Pyewacket isn't with me. She didn't want to come so I didn't insist. Sometimes she gets car sick. Also, she's been talking with the other familiars about establishing a union. They want to limit the number of seances per week, or else they'll strike. I don't know all the details because she's being rather standoffish about the whole thing. Frankly, I don't think I make her work too hard."

"Familiars want to unionize? I've never heard of that before," said Monica with an arched eyebrow.

"Yes, Pyewacket wants more benefits and time off for all the holidays including St. Patrick's Day. She has some Leprechaun friends and likes to drink green milk and dance the night away with them. Personally, I think they're a bad lot. In addition, the union wants to establish a Be Kind to Cats Day, too. And that's not all."

"What else?"

"They want paternity leave in addition to maternity leave. Where will it end?"

Monica didn't know what to say about the situation. "I'm sure Pyewacket has very good working conditions in your house. She doesn't need to join a union."

"I gave her more than her usual amount of catnip before I left. If I could keep her away from Tuffy, the familiar union organizer, she might forget about the whole thing. Whenever she talks with him, she gets all fired up." Llorona shrugged her shoulders.

"Can you still contact the ghost without her?" asked Monica.

"Yes, but I'll have to use a different channel." The seer immediately got right down to business. "Where is the death spot? I need to prepare the area."

Monica didn't waste time and quickly led her to the place on stage where they had replaced the blood soaked boards with new ones. She stepped back while pointing to The Spot and said, "That's where they found him."

From inside her tote, Llorona took out a stick of incense and ten black candles with their holders. After placing the candles in a circle around the area of the death, she put the incense in the center. She took out a Bic lighter and lit all of them. Immediately an intense spicy smell pervaded the atmosphere.

She asked Hugh to turn out the stage lights. The flickering candles made shadowy figures on the walls and caused crummy visibility.

Muttering indistinguishable syllables, the seer circled the gloomy tableau. The bystanders politely remained attentive until the stage door opened. Milt and Meredith barged in, slammed the door, tramped across the stage, and in general made an obtrusive amount of noise. Llorona stopped chanting while delivering a frosty scowl to the newcomers.

While Llorona returned to her ritual, Milt sidled over to Hugh. Although Milt put his hand partly over his mouth, his vibrant voice carried. "I heard there was going to be a seance by this voodoo priestess, and since she's trying to summon the spirit of my brother, I feel I should be here."

"Of course, you're welcome, " said Hugh in hushed tones. "Llorona is going to speak with the dead in order to find out who has been making all the disturbances that have affected the singers. The goal, of course, is to produce a good opera."

Since Monica heard the conversation, she was sure Llorona heard it too. She wondered if the oracle was offended by the term *voodoo priestess.* Monica got her answer when she peered at Llorona who was narrowing her cold eyes at the brash intruder.

Meredith didn't remain silent either. She whispered loudly to her husband, "Let's hope this doesn't take long, or we're going to be late for our dinner at mother's. She hates it when we're late. Besides, my salad could go limp in the car while we're here."

Llorona put a finger to her lips shushing the rude talkers. Chastened, the group of spectators kept quiet. Llorona continued chanting and pacing in a circle.

As Monica peeped at the faces, she noticed only Belinda was intently watching the seer with conviction. Meredith took obvious looks at her watch. Hugh used his tongue to remove a piece of food stuck on a back tooth. Milt rocked back and forth in his shoes with his thumbs in his pants pockets. Monica waited expectantly for a good flimflam show.

During the mumbling of the chant, Monica tried to hear familiar Latin words since she had studied Latin in high school. But she couldn't distinguish any words like *amo, amas, amat, or pax*. Was Latin the language of the dead? Since it was a dead language, maybe it made sense, sort of.

Nothing spectacular was happening. Llorona just kept creeping around in a circle while croaking her indistinguishable words.

Like a bolt of lightening, a gust of wind extinguished the candles. In unison Milt and Hugh said, "What the hell?"

Without the candle light, Monica could see nothing, not even shapes. Llorona howled out, "Ahaa" which began on a high note and descended dramatically. Monica felt little prickles along her backbone.

Hugh spoke out, "I have a little flashlight in my pocket. Just a minute, folks." Monica heard scratchy noises as he dug around in his jacket. In a few seconds, she heard a click sound and saw a tiny circle of light swooping around the stage as Hugh walked to the light switch and turned it on.

Everyone started to ask questions at once.

"What happened?"

"Where did that gust come from?"

"Did someone open the stage door and come in?" There were no answers.

Monica walked back and found the stage door shut. She didn't find any explanation for the gust of wind that blew out the candles.

When she looked at Hugh, he shrugged his shoulders and said, "I don't know what happened. The door is closed, and I don't see any fans. I haven't the slightest idea what blew out the candles."

While people were looking about, Llorona gathered up the partly used candles and the incense, put them in her tote, and headed for the door. Her mouth was in a grim line.

Monica walked over to her and asked, "Did the spirit blow out the candles?"

The fortune-teller wheezed, "I must leave. I will take no money." She hurriedly left without any explanation.

The others watched her go but didn't ask why she was leaving. Monica felt tongue-tied, too. When Monica had her previous dealings with Llorora, the fortune-teller had been pleasant and accommodating. Why was she having a snit now?

Monica shook off an ominous feeling and went back to being a reasonable person. "Maybe she got angry because we weren't quiet," she said. She tried to lighten the atmosphere by adding, "I hoped to see a good show."

Hugh said, "On the financial side, I just saved $100."

Meredith grabbed her husband's arm and hurried him toward the door. "What a waste of time. We're late for mother's dinner."

Belinda showed some concern. "I'm scared. I think the spirit did come and for some reason frightened Llorona. Maybe I'll call her later, but not now."

Everyone walked out the stage door. After Hugh locked it, he tested the knob a couple times to be sure it was secure. The disconcerted group dispersed in various directions with just a few calls, "See you Monday."

While driving home, Monica turned her thoughts to her evening meeting with Rick. Perhaps he could provide insight into the phantom affair.

As Monica prepared her apartment for her visitor, her cats chased each other from room to room. After their game, both of them flopped down on the sofa and washed their faces. Monica sat down next to them. She stroked Marilyn with her right hand and Bob with her left since she felt the importance of always being fair and giving each one the same attention.

Before returning to her domestic duties, she reminded Bob of his mission. "Have you found my pearl necklace yet? Pyewacket said you could find it." Bob purred loudly.

When Rick arrived, Monica opened the door and said, "Come in, come in. I just finished cutting the pie."

After she scooped the vanilla ice cream on top of two pieces of homemade cherry pie, she said, "Tonight was really interesting. Let's sit down in the living room. While we're eating our pie, I'll tell you all about it."

Monica tucked one leg under her as she sat on the sofa, still occupied by two cats. Before even picking up her fork, she gave Rick her report on the evening's happenings.

Rick attacked his dessert with gusto. "Good pie," said Rick as he licked a stray piece of cherry from the corner of his mouth.

"But what do you think about the strange gust of wind, Llorona's leaving without collecting her money, and the ghost?" asked Monica who wanted his unbiased opinion.

"Quite a dustup," he said.

"A dustup? It was more than a dustup. A dustup is a trivial thing," declared Monica with conviction as she held a piece of pie on her fork Mitsey, her mixed breed dog, sat near the sofa and looked hungrily at the quivering piece of crust that could fall at any minute.

Rick swallowed more pie before he suggested an explanation. "Perhaps she had an accomplice who opened the stage door enough to let the wind in and then closed it quickly. You spectators are convinced the ghost is present and might cause problems. When you beg her to come back, she'll double or triple her fee."

Monica grinned. "That's the best answer I've heard. I believe Belinda will beg her to come back no matter what the fee is."

Rick laughed and in a moment of expansiveness fed Mitsey a sizeable piece of crust. Rick and Mitsey had become good friends during the past few months. Mitsey always sat near him when food was involved since she always received good treats from this dog loving visitor every time he came.

Monica admired Mitsey's technique for begging. She didn't bark annoyingly or scratch legs, but she made her eyes soft, loving, and pitiful. She positioned her nose at a becoming angle, drooped her head in a humble way, and gazed soulfully like a waif who hasn't eaten in days. Rick broke off another crumb of crust for her.

"Now, Ms. Jessica Fletcher, you have more mysteries to solve," added Rick. "Finding the killer of Rob Grainger is the biggest one." Rick crossed his long legs and stretched out his arms over his head.

"Tell me more details about his death. I've read the newspaper account, but you must have more information," said Monica.

"Rob had just finished performing the play *Blithe Spirit* that evening. After the play, a number of the audience members went on stage to congratulate the actors. Later, the cast went to the Hairy Ape Bar to party."

Monica had heard about the party before. "Did anyone stay behind?"

"Joe Barney, the set designer and stage hand, stayed at the theater to do some work. He repaired a bookcase, touched up a few spots that needed paint, and piled a few boxes in the back. While he was doing this work, he didn't see anyone or hear any noise. He thought he was alone in the theater although he didn't check the dressing rooms or any other part of the theater since it wasn't his job. About 11:30 he left."

"Where was Rob during that time?" asked Monica as she spooned the last of the vanilla ice cream in her mouth.

"No one knows. He never arrived at the bar. The next morning the janitors found his body with a dagger in his back on center stage. He had been stabbed three times. The killer left the dagger in the body after the last thrust. No fingerprints on the fancy handle of the dagger which had been used in several plays and kept in the prop room."

"I would love to solve that crime," taunted Monica as she gave Rick a flirtatious smile.

"Well, you know Miss Marple always outsmarted Scotland Yard," said Rick with a grin. "Let's see if you can beat the Albuquerque Police Department in finding the killer."

"I take that as a challenge," Monica replied as she leaned over and kissed Rick. While the kissing was going on, Mitsey put her two front paws on the coffee table and cleaned both plates of all residue of ice cream and pie. A good end to the evening for all.

6

When everyone assembled for rehearsal on Monday night, Hugh announced, "I have a big surprise. I got a call from *Spook Finders,* the television show that investigates haunted locales of any sort. The producer heard of our situation here at the Kimo Theater and wants to do an entire 30 minute show about our ghost. Since we're doing an opera, he can tie his spook hunting to the musical, *The Phantom of the Opera*. He says it should draw millions of viewers."

The entire cast clapped while grinning broadly. Monica could hear the happy shouts, "We're going to be on TV!"

"Let's do the 'Habanera' number. It's the most popular song in the opera," suggested Belinda.

Under her breath, Monica whispered to Leslie, "And guess who sings it?"

After a few minutes of excitement, Hugh quieted them down. "The producer said he wants to film enactments of the discoveries of the black roses by the two principals and probably something dealing with the broken legs on the tavern bar. The crew will arrive here tomorrow."

Meredith whined, "I threw my rose away."

"I kept mine," boasted Belinda. "I imagine he'll want to film me, not only as the lead singer, but also as the recipient of the evil black rose."

"Do you think they'll want to redo the scene in which I lean against the tavern bar, and it collapses?"

asked Burt Brown. "I could have broken my leg and been forced to sing while on crutches. I could have lost my voice from infection after injuring any part of my body. It was a hideous trick of the ghost or whatever." Burt had a worry frown on his face.

"They aren't going to redo the breaking of the tavern bar," reassured Monica. The prop men don't want to repair the legs of another bar. Also, don't worry about germs. You look like the picture of health. No germ will get near you." Monica looked at Burt's barrel chest and strong limbs while she made her statement. No one else appeared to be listening to Burt's whiny fears.

Hugh said, "This production is going to sell out." He raised both arms with his thumbs up as he shouted out the good news.

The cast burst into song, "For he's a jolly good gho-ost, For he's a jolly good gho-ost, For he's a jolly good gho-ost, Which nobody can deny." People slapped each other on the back and smacked their hands in high fives.

"Be sure and remember any little thing connected to the ghost," advised Hugh. "Write down any object that was moved mysteriously." Monica noted Hugh's change from pooh-poohing the spook theory to professing a belief in it.

"I couldn't find my pink lipstick the other night. Later, I found it in the Green Room," said Meredith.

"For God's sake, Meredith, you just misplaced your old lipstick. Let's not fabricate incidents," snapped Milt. "The producer of *Spook Finders* doesn't want junk like that. I'm sure he wants black roses, falling lights, and broken furniture. Too bad we can't replicate the falling of the chandelier." Milt looked up at the ceiling which now had a plain globe light fixture.

A number of voices expressed hope the ghost would do something spectacular when the TV crew arrived.

Monica wondered what methods the crew would use to find this so-called phantom of the opera. If they didn't find a spook, would the producer cancel the Albuquerque show?

While the cast members speculated about the future, Monica sought out Joe who was on his knees painting some boards for the tavern scene. "Anything to report?" she asked.

"Nothing. I came a little early tonight, but I didn't see any of my stuff moved. I can't believe how this TV show has gotten people worked up. There isn't any ghost."

Monica hunkered down beside him. "I agree with you. We have a flesh and blood person causing these mishaps. By the way, were you working *Blithe Spirit* on the night Rob was killed?"

"Yup, I was. You know that Rob was a good-looking guy. The women hung around him all the time, listened to every word he said, and laughed at his stupid jokes. According to the cast gossip, he was dating a singer who lived in town, but no one had any real information."

"Do you know why he came back to Albuquerque? I heard after graduating from the University of New Mexico, he went to New York where he became a successful actor." Monica thought it was odd he returned to his hometown if he were flourishing in the Big Apple.

Joe kept slapping on blue paint. "I chatted with him a couple times, and he said after working in New York, he needed to take a break."

Joe paused and put his brush in the paint can as he reminisced about the murdered Rob. "That night I was the last one in the theater. I put away the props, repaired a few things, and touched up some paint. If someone had been there, I would have heard a noise. I didn't hear anything."

Monica said, "I think Rob had a key. From what I've observed there are a lot of loose keys. But if he did have a key, why would he come back to the theater, and why was he on the stage when his assailant stabbed him?" Monica wondered how Jessica Fletcher or Stephanie Plum would approach these questions.

Hugh shook her out of her revere when he made an announcement, "Ladies, gentlemen, let's continue rehearsing. We'll start with the tavern scene."

Still gossiping, the members of the cast found their spots, the orchestra began to play, and the beautiful music of Bizet filled the theater.

After the rehearsal ended, Monica and Leslie collected their jackets and purses which they had piled on a chair. While Monica stuck her arm in the sleeve of her blazer, she muttered to Leslie, "Who would want to scare Burt? He's such a big wuss. What's fun about scaring someone who already sees a possible tragedy in just walking across the street?"

"Burt is so annoying when he whines. I think it's the ghost's way of punishing the entire cast," answered Leslie as she wrapped a black woven shawl over her shoulders.

Nick, the other prop man, walked over and spoke to them as they headed toward the door. "I heard you talking to Joe about Rob. I sure hope they find his killer. We were both on the football team in high school. Rob was a darn good athlete in all sports, not at all like his fat, little brother who was a real nerd. Now, Milt looks good after he lost weight in college."

"I didn't know Milt had been a nerd in high school," said Monica.

"He was a fat nerd, and his brother was a good-looking, star athlete. What a contrast to have in the same family," mused Nick. "Things have changed. Look at Milt now."

Monica turned and saw Milt chatting with several girls from the chorus. They smiled at him while he expressed his ideas on *Spook Finders*. One of his arms snaked around the waist of a young college girl who seemed very engrossed in what he was saying.

"Nick, were you working the night Rob died?" asked Monica.

"Yes. I had a headache and decided to leave after the curtain came down. I remember one funny thing that happened just before I left. As I walked out the door, Madam Arcati removed her wig, threw it on the floor, and called it a rat. Everyone laughed. Of course, they were all in high spirits because the theater had been fully booked, and the audience had clapped long and loud."

"Did they plan to party somewhere?"

"Sure. They were going to the Hairy Ape Bar. I heard later Rob never got there."

"Maybe he planned on meeting someone here in the theater," speculated Monica. Leslie tugged on her sleeve. Monica got the point and moved towards the door. "Thanks guys," she called out.

Just outside the door, Monica overheard Burt Brown talking with Belinda. "I just know the producer will want to reenact the scene of the collapsing tavern bar. I could crack my elbow and never be able to lift a glass again." He ran his hand up and down his right arm.

"Just don't lean on it. Pretend you're leaning on it," advised Belinda. "If you keep your balance on both feet, you won't fall."

"Okay, I won't lean. I'll just rest my hand on it." Burt spread out his arm and tested some gestures of possible use for the dreaded scene.

"I know they'll want to film me finding the black flower. I'll try to recapture my exact emotions when I saw it lying there on the top of my dresser. I hope they film part of the opera itself, especially when I sing the 'Habanera' since it's the showcase aria." Belinda broke into the song as she left Burt and headed for her car.

Monica caught the conversation of Milt and Meredith Grainger as they walked past her. Meredith said to her husband, "Surely they'll film the scene when I enter the smugglers' lair to talk to Joseimus about his dying mother. I love that aria."

Milt talked about his role of Joseimus as he walked. "This complex character is torn between his passion for Carmen and his life in the little village with his mother and Flavia. It takes a superb performer to sing and act out this constant struggle. I'm sure the producer will film one of those scenes where I demonstrate the tortured conscience of Joseimus."

As Monica drove home, she wondered if the producer would have more trouble with the living than with the dead.

The next morning Monica picked up the newspaper from her front door and immediately saw the screaming headlines about the ghost at the Kimo Theater. She took the paper with her to school, but most of the teachers had already read it. Many of them planned to make reservations for the opera. As Hugh had predicted earlier, a haunted theater boosted sales.

Before her last class, Hugh walked into Monica's room with a big smile on his face and excitedly spit out his new plans. "I'm going to add another performance. I checked, and the theater is available. I'm sure the singers will want to do the extra show. This phantom business is great."

"What if you find out a teenage boy is the prankster?" asked Monica who hated to burst his bubble, but it could happen.

"I'm hoping it doesn't happen until the show is over. Frankly, I'm going to play along and pretend a ghost is responsible for all the strange activities. And, Monica, I'd appreciate it if you would do the same," said Hugh.

"Why not?" agreed Monica. "For the good of the show, I'll keep my mouth shut. Do you think the producer will want to bring in our local oracle for more atmosphere?" While she chatted with Hugh, Monica multi-tasked. She took a late paper from a student, put away several stray paper clips, and assembled her handouts for her next class.

"He might want to include Llorona. When I talked to him on the phone, he showed interest in her. He plans on filming rehearsals, enactments of paranormal activity, interviews with cast members, and scenes from opening night. Of course, if anything newsworthy happens, he'll add it on the spot." Hugh's eyes twinkled as he spoke about having his opera on a national TV program.

Monica, too, felt it would be fun to be on TV even if she was only in the chorus. Maybe she'd get a new haircut. Hugh gave Monica a pat on the back before he rushed out just as the bell rang.

Although Monica's students were all in their chairs, they were not getting out books. They were talking with their friends and showing each other pictures on their phones. When Monica began class with the usual, "Please, take out your literature books." They made exaggerated sighing noises like this request was an onerous burden in their lives.

Today, they were going to study the tone of one of Henry's speeches in William Shakespeare's *Henry V*. Days before, the students had enacted the battle scene. Now they would analyze the language.

Monica said, "Students, we'll start with Henry's battle cry. 'Once more unto the breach, dear friends, once more,/ Or close the wall up with our English dead!'" As she spoke those stirring words, she felt the young king's courage as he faced a much larger French army.

Instead of reading the entire speech herself, she chose a student in the last row. As he stumbled over the lines, Monica daydreamed. She would confront the delinquent, the murderer, or any other evildoer at the theater and be like the lionhearted Henry. From her heroic thoughts, she descended to the egotistical. She really wanted to beat the police in finding out whodunit.

7

Since Monica arrived early, she saw the TV crew hit the theater like the troops landing on Omaha beach. They brought in machines, microphones, cameras, and infrared lights. They carried ladders and positioned their digital surveillance cameras on the stage, behind the stage, in the dressing rooms, and in the seating area.

When the cast arrived, all the equipment had been installed. Instead of rehearsal clothes consisting of old tired jeans and faded tee shirts, tonight the cast members wore spiffy shirts, sweaters with color coordinated scarves, and matching turquoise necklaces and earrings.

Monica noticed new haircuts, freshly shampooed hair, and sparkling fingernail polish with glued on sequins. She, too, had taken extra care with her appearance and wore her jeans with bling on the pockets and a new white turtleneck sweater.

Before the rehearsal, Hugh called everyone on stage and introduced Cap Slater, the producer of *Spook Finders*. Cap reminded Monica of a pudgy bulldog since he had a broad face, wide shoulders, and assertive manner.

Cap strutted to the microphone and said, "Hello, everyone. I'm glad we could be here to help you with your ghost problem. Just go about your business and forget we're here. We'll do our work, find that spook, and exorcise him. We plan to make a 30 minute TV show that will air probably in a month or so. As I said before, forget we're here. Just do what you normally do."

After the loud clapping ended, Cap surveyed the stage while he conferred with his crew. As Monica watched, the well-dressed Belinda pranced by in her high heels. Hugh fiddled with a blue ascot he wore with his striped shirt. Bert, in his Spartacus attire, struck a pose in which he inflated his chest, stood with his legs apart, and grasped his spear in one hand and his shield in another. Just a normal rehearsal.

Hugh called for the final scene in which Carmen goes to the Roman games where she shows her preference for Spartacus, rather than Joseimus. After getting into position, the principals began the scene. Milt, as Joseimus, sang of his love for Carmen and pleaded with her to go with him. Belinda, as Carmen, refused his entreaty.

Angry because she had ditched him, Joseimus pushed her to the floor, leaned over her, took out his stage dagger with the retractable blade and thrust it between Carmen's chest and her arm as rehearsed as a safety measure. Instead of retracting, the blade hit the floor and went in about an inch. Milt stopped singing and pushed the dagger against the stage floor several times to test it, but it didn't retract.

The action stopped. "This isn't the stage dagger. This is a real dagger!" shouted Milt. Immediately the camera man did a close up of Milt holding the dagger high in the air. "My God! Who did this?"

Cassandra answered, "The phantom of the opera."

Monica thought she shouldn't say anything about the possibility of a flesh and blood prankster as Cap and his crew took action. Monica watched from the side as Cap urged another camera man to zoom in.

Belinda stood up, put her hand on her throat, and proclaimed, "The ghost wants to kill me! I am the target. But why? He sent me the black rose as a warning and now the dagger." The camera man switched to Belinda who kept repeating, "The ghost wants me dead!"

Monica noted that Belinda arched her back in a very becoming way as she proclaimed her dire future. The cast watched this drama with wide-opened eyes and mouths.

"Belinda, darling, let me get you a cup of tea," consoled Hugh as he put his arm around her. "I won't let anything happen to you," he promised.

Joe, the prop man, rushed on stage. "I took the stage dagger from the exact same spot where it's always kept. I didn't test it. Why should I? It's the retractable dagger we've been using," he explained. He grabbed the dagger from Milt and examined it. A bit of metal was jammed by the blade to prevent it from retracting. "Someone sabotaged it," he exclaimed.

The camera men switched from one person to another. Cap's eyes glittered as he gave directions to his crew. Monica heard him say under his breath, "God, this is great! I'm catching the action as it happens."

Belinda raised her arms high in the air and shouted, "Ghost, where are you? Why do you want to kill me?" Her vibrant voice resounded as she tossed her hair back.

Milt lifted his fist and shook it. He proclaimed, "I'll get you for this!" His feet were firmly planted on the floor while his arm and clenched fist shook in his defiance of this treacherous spook. "I don't want anyone to say this was done by my brother's spirit!"

"Is this the same dagger that killed Rob Grainger?" asked Cap. His question wasn't directed at any one person.

Milt dropped the dagger with a clang. "Could this be the same dagger that killed my beloved brother? Too cruel, too cruel," he cried as he slumped and sat down heavily on a chair. "How can I go on with this show?" he wailed.

Hugh rushed over to Milt. "It'll be okay. I'm sure the police still have the other dagger in their evidence room. Let me get you a cup of tea."

The cameras rolled, spotlights illuminated the speakers, and men moved microphones to get the best sound. After filming the hysterical scene, Cap looked around for another drama, but nothing else happened.

The cast members talked together in small groups but later moved towards the stage door to go home. There was only so much to say about the dagger. Joe pried out the piece of metal from the dagger and oiled the retraction lever as he showed it to Cap.

The evening ended when Cap announced, "We're going to find that spook and kick him out of the theater."

On the front page of the Albuquerque Journal the next morning the headline said, "*Spook Finders* Pledge to Remove Spook from the Kimo." After reading the morning paper, Monica called Hugh. "How is Cap planning to get rid of the ghost? Is Llorona going to return?"

Hugh said, "I have no idea, but the publicity is great. I've gotten calls from all sorts of people who are asking questions about ghosts, exorcisms, and the opera. I heard a crowd of kids peeked through the little windows in the doors of the Kimo. Several tried to open the doors, but, of course, they were locked. Albuquerque has a thirst for a haunted theater. We'll have sellouts every night."

"I'm glad," said Monica. "I'll continue to forget about any rational talk about a live prankster."

"Thanks, Monica. See you tonight," said Hugh.

When Monica came to the stage door for rehearsal, some eager beaver teenagers tried to squeeze in, but Pops held them back.

Just like the night before, the members of the company looked great. The women wore heels with their designer jeans, and the men sported new polo shirts. Monica had buckled under the enticement of being on TV and bought more new clothes. She wore new jeans and a Scandinavian style red sweater.

While tucking in his new green ascot into the collar of his white shirt, Hugh walked to center stage and called them together for a ghost report.

Cap strode forward and spoke to the hushed group. "Sorry folks, we don't have any more news about this spook. We had motion sensors all over the stage and back areas, but nothing tripped them off during the night. Don't worry, we'll find that ghost and get rid of him."

Although Cap spoke with confidence, bordering on cockiness, Cassandra wasn't convinced. "The phantom won't leave until his mission is over. Evil will return."

Monica was getting tired of Cassandra's freaky prophecies. She decided if Burt and Cassandra ever got together, they could depress even a kid with a new puppy.

Cap ignored Cassandra. He just got down to business by taking out his clipboard. "I would like to film Belinda and Meredith finding the black roses. Do you girls think you could remember your emotions when you saw the flowers?"

Both nodded. Meredith added, "I threw my flower away."

Cap replied, "We'll just use Belinda's flower for both scenes. That's okay with you, isn't it Belinda?"

Belinda smiled sweetly. "Of course, it is. I'll be glad to share my flower with her."

Cap turned towards Hugh. "If you don't mind, we'll take a few minutes to shoot each of the girls finding the black rose. It shouldn't hold up your rehearsal for very long."

"Okay, we'll rehearse another scene now with the smugglers," said Hugh smiling pleasantly.

Instead of chatting, Monica wanted to watch the discovery scenes with the two flower recipients so she stepped behind the camera guy as he went into the dressing room that both women shared.

Cap filmed Belinda first. She walked over to her place at the dressing table, saw the flower, squeaked a tiny bit, touched the rose, and dropped it as if it were a hot poker. "What is this? What does it mean? Does the ghost want to kill me?" she shrieked as she pushed her arms out as if to ward off the specter.

Monica would have rolled her eyes, but she feared someone would catch a glimpse of her cheeky gesture.

Cap asked Belinda to repeat the action twice more. Monica thought every time she did it, she screeched in a higher octave, and her arm movements became grander.

When Meredith's turn came, she downplayed the scene. She walked over to her spot at the dressing table, furrowed her brow, picked up the flower, and hissed, "What's this ugly flower doing here?" She tossed it in the trash can as if it were a nasty, dirty insect. Cap had her go over her discovery scene several times, too.

Afterwards, Monica saw a triumphant gleam in the eyes of both women as they returned to the stage.

Before they rehearsed the final scene, Hugh showed how the dagger had been repaired by pushing the blade inside the hilt several times. Hugh added, "When Milt uses the dagger, he still will stick it between her chest and arm so there will be no bruising. But the dagger is retracting, folks."

The cast went though the last scene. At the point where Joseimus stabs Carmen, Monica heard a few sharp intakes of breath. Joseimus raised his arm and thrust the dagger just where it was supposed to be. The blade retracted, but from the audience's point of view, it looked like a real death blow.

The dying Carmen lay on the floor in an attractive pose showing a lot of thigh. After Joseimus says his last words, "I have killed her! Oh, Carmen! My beloved Carmen," the music came to a flourishing end.

Cap announced, "I filmed the final scene with the repaired dagger as well as the discovery of the altered dagger. I'll be using those segments for my show." This statement brought out big smiles and twinkling eyes on the entire cast. Monica thought being on TV had improved everyone's outlook on life.

"Wonderful, wonderful," shouted Hugh with a big grin on his face.

Belinda whispered to Milt, "How was my reaction when I realized the dagger was real? Was my voice too high pitched?"

"You were perfect, just the right amount of worry and concern for the danger in your life. Your acting ability is wonderful, my dear." While Milt praised Belinda, he circled her waist with his arm. "How did I do?"

"You were magnificent."

Monica decided the rose and jig controversy had been forgotten since Belinda and Milt appeared to be getting along very well indeed. Monica switched her thoughts to Cap and wondered what he had in mind for the rest of his show. She ambled over to him while he was adjusting a wall camera.

"Mr. Slater, I'm Monica Walters. I'd like to offer my help in any way I can. I've lived here in Albuquerque all my life so I can give you local information if you need any," said Monica as she stood by his side.

"Thank you, Monica. Please call me Cap. I might need to ask you a few questions later. I just got the background about Rob. Milt told me his dead brother isn't the phantom of the opera. He said his actor brother loved the theater and would never do anything to sabotage a production. Do you have an opinion?"

Cap took out a cigarette and put it to his lips. When Monica shook her head in a negative fashion, he returned it to his crumpled pack.

"I didn't know Rob Grainger, but it seems he doesn't have a motive for scaring people," answered Monica. As she was talking to Cap, she noticed several people staring at a fuzzy spiral of smoke. "Is something on fire?" she asked while sniffing the air.

Cap looked in her direction, saw the smoke, and shouted happily, "It's the spook!"

Everyone stopped talking and gawked at the spot. The spirals of smoke kept moving upwards without any indication of fire.

Several voices said in unison, "The phantom is back."

Camera men, sound men, and other crew members rushed forward with their equipment. While Cap gave directions for filming from different angles, the lights went out. A loud whooshing sound followed the loss of light. The smoke phenomena hadn't scared anyone, but the darkness and whoosh did.

A couple women yelped, a few tittered nervously, and one man shouted, "What the hell happened to the lights?"

Monica felt a hand snake around her waist and a vibrant voice crooned, "You're the prettiest girl here."

Monica recognized the unmistakable voice of the opera's tenor. Monica could feel Milt's warm breath on her cheek as he tried to find her lips. Quickly she coughed and pretended to sneeze. " I'm getting a cold," she squeaked.

"A cold!" Milt's hand left her waist, his head snapped back, and he jerked his feet away and bumped into some other person. The lights went on, and Monica saw Milt squirting the air around her with an antiseptic spray. She decided he must keep a little bottle in his pocket because she had seen him squirt door knobs before.

Apparently no one really cared what Milt was doing since they all were chattering about the funny smoke and the lights going off. Several voices spoke out.

"What happened?"

"Did the ghost do that?"

"What was that noise?"

Monica sneezed again just for fun. Milt jumped away even father from her.

This little attempt at a stolen kiss had gotten her attention away from the spook caper. Monica figured a person turned off the lights, but the smoke thing and the funny sound she didn't understand. She'd call Rick when she got home. He could always come up with some very human method of making paranormal imitations.

After the chaos, Cap called the cast together and said cheerfully, "We'll be here all night. Don't worry, folks. We'll get that spook." He rubbed his hands together while his eyes danced.

Cap's pleasure seemed to rub off on the cast because all their remarks were about the fortuitous return of the phantom.

"He's back."

"I hope I was in that last shot."

"Maybe he'll stay for the run of the show."

The rehearsal ended with high spirits and an anticipation of a full house for all the performances of the opera including the extra one.

8

As Monica talked to people at school and at the grocery store, she heard positive comments about the ghost at the theater. He became a friendly being, like Casper in the cartoon. A ghost scampering around the old Kimo Theater tickled the imagination and made Albuquerque a more exciting place.

On the good financial side, the box office booked many reservations for the opera which opened the next weekend.

Monday night when Monica and Leslie arrived at the theater, four students paraded in a picket line with placards which said, "Ghosts Have Rights" and "Don't Kick Out Our Spook." Cap filmed them as they walked back and forth. People chuckled when they passed by, and a couple cars honked.

"What kind of a crazy protest is this?" asked Monica.

"They don't want the ghost evicted," howled Leslie.

With big grins on their faces, Monica and Leslie watched the parading protestors. Monica squinted her eyes and said, "That's Leroy Marx. He's a student at the University, and the last time I saw him he was protesting the peace movement."

"Leroy," she called out. Leroy dropped his sign and ambled over to speak to her.

"Hi, Miss Walters, I want to save the ghost from eviction," he announced.

"Do you feel he's being treated unfairly? Is this a case of ghost abuse?" she asked while trying to keep a straight face.

"Oh, yes. This is his or her home. Why should he or she have to leave it?" said Leroy solemnly. Monica noted he was very careful about not showing any gender bias. He removed his baseball cap that he wore with the bill on the back and wiped his forehead with the back of his hands. His jeans had holes, and the sleeves had been ripped off his tee shirt.

Monica noted he had put on a little weight since she last saw him. His chubby cheeks gave him a cherubic look.

Monica decided to refer to the ghost as a male. "Maybe he isn't happy here. Maybe he wants to find a better place to live, like in a mausoleum or a graveyard," suggested Monica playing along with the idea of doing what is best for the spook. Leslie, who was standing next to her, arched an eyebrow.

The other protestors had been listening to the conversation and lined up with Leroy who firmly said, "It should be his choice. If he wants to leave, he'll leave. No one should be forced out of his home." Leroy had switched to the masculine pronoun instead of the awkward *he* or *she* combination.

The other protestors chimed in, "We believe in choice."

Monica grinned and said, "Okay, you've got a point."

Leroy added, "The Save the Whale people are coming tomorrow and maybe the Tofu for Thanksgiving crowd, too. We're going to win!" he shouted and raised his free arm high. The others let their signs droop on their left arms and raised their right ones.

One of the protestors timidly asked Cap, "Are we going to be on TV?"

"Yes, indeed, this is first-rate stuff. You'll all be in the program," he promised. Smiles broke out. They resumed their parade with a jaunty gait.

When Monica and Leslie got back in the theater for the rehearsal, Burt spoke to Monica, "Did you see those idiots out there? What poppycock! *They* think the ghost is cute. It's a malevolent spirit. I could have twisted my back, thrown my neck out of kilter, and screwed up my voice. They don't know what I've been through," Burt wailed.

Meredith joined the group and said in a worried voice, "I hope Cap doesn't spend all his time out there with those morons. He should be filming back here, on stage." Meredith pursed her lips and squinted her eyes.

Milt bellowed out, "What a cockamamy bunch of imbeciles. Call the police. Arrest them for trespassing or whatever." Milt paced back and forth across the stage while repeating the same words.

He hunted up Hugh and demanded, "Do something! Get rid of those blockheads."

Hugh replied in a tired, exasperated tone, "They're college students so any minute they could leave to go back to the dorm to study."

In contrast to the principals' annoyance, the cast members snickered, and a few roared with merriment. Monica decided the protestors seeking help for the allegedly abused spook made all the past incidents amusing rather than scary.

After blowing his whistle for attention, Hugh announced, "These young people will soon get tired of carrying those heavy signs around. Don't worry, they'll go away, and besides, the publicity will bring in more ticket sales."

After a brief pause, he said, "Tonight we'll work on the last act. Tomorrow night we'll go through the whole show with all the tech. Dress rehearsal the next night, dark on Thursday, and on Friday it's opening night."

Everyone clapped and cheered. Even Milt stopped huffing. The TV crew set up a camera facing the stage and immediately Monica noticed the members of the cast were running combs through their hair, tucking in shirts, and applying lip gloss. The hyperactive Cap bounced around as he checked various pieces of equipment and conferred with his crew.

Everything stopped when suddenly the lights went off, and a fake falsetto voice sobbed, "I don't want to go. I like it here. Stop abusing me." Lots of guffawing followed. The lights went back on, and Monica saw the drummer and the short clarinet player bent over with laughter.

"Now, folks, let's cut out the hijinks," said Hugh although his eyes danced and the corners of his mouth lifted as he held back a grin.

The lights went off again. Everyone waited, and the same fake voice said, "I don't take up much space. I'm an airy fairy." Lights went back on. The drummer and clarinet player roared again while the French horn player got caught with his finger on the light switch.

Hugh said, "That's enough. That's enough. Joe, will you stand guard over the light switch tonight, or we're not going to get anything done."

Still whooping it up, the orchestra members trudged down into the pit. Even Meredith, Milt, and Burt, the three grumpy complainers, had snickered at the antics. Monica and Leslie, along with the cast, laughed and enjoyed the joke tremendously.

The Act IV stage set, the plaza outside the Colosseum where the gladiators would fight, had large pillars and stone benches. The orchestra conductor lifted his baton, and music filled the house. The dancers twirled while the chorus sang about the glory of the games.

When Spartacus and Carmen entered together as a couple, one of the gypsy girls approached Carmen and warned her of the presence of the jealous Joseimus. The singing petered out after Joseimus missed his cue and didn't come on stage.

Hugh became annoyed and shouted, "Joseimus, you're on. Milt, Milt you're on." No sound of running feet or any feet at all.. "Someone go get him," he barked.

Cassandra, the closest cast member to the dressing rooms, said, "I'll go." As she walked, she shouted his name a few times. After a few moments, everyone heard a high pitched scream, and Cassandra ran back to the stage. "He's on the floor. The evil phantom did something to him."

Hugh, the quickest on his feet, made it to the dressing room first. Monica followed him. Milt was lying down on his back. His foot twitched a bit, so Monica knew he was alive. Hugh knelt down, touched Milt on the shoulder, and helped him sit up. Milt shook his head like he was shaking water out of his ears at a swimming pool.

Hugh asked him, "Are you okay? What happened?"

"It was very strange. I heard this eerie sound, high and breathy, like it was coming through a fog. It said, 'Beware.' It was definitely a female voice. I saw a figure, a female, in a mist who pushed me down. After that I must have been unconscious because I don't remember anything until Cassandra screamed."

Milt rubbed the back of his head and added, "I don't feel a lump."

Meredith rushed over to him, bent down, and threw her arms around his neck. "Darling, are you all right? Are you sure, my love?" Meredith helped her husband struggle to his feet. Both pairs of eyes took a quick glance to see where the camera was.

As Milt scrambled up, he smoothed his hair and lifted his chin. Monica knew actors wanted to avoid neck wrinkles. With her arms around her husband's shoulders, Meredith raised her head, turned slightly, and spoke more to the camera than to Milt, "Darling, I'm so glad you're alive. That evil spirit could have killed you."

Hugh asked, "Did you say a female spirit pushed you?"

"Yes, it was frightful. She came at me in a mist. It's hard to describe , but she had evil eyes that stared into my very soul," explained Milt. "Why did she choose me? Perhaps it's because I play Joseimus, the male lead."

"I should be worried since I play Flavia," pointed out Meredith who no longer made any attempt to look at Milt, but zeroed in directly on the camera.

" But *I* am the principal of the opera. I should be the one who should be concerned because I have the most important role. *I* am Carmen," chimed in Belinda who swirled her hair so that two curls flipped attractively over her neck while she lifted her chin.

After her pronouncement, she sighed as if she carried the burden of the world on her shoulders.

"From now on, let's go everywhere in groups or at least in pairs. I think you all will feel safer if you aren't alone," suggested Hugh. In an attempt to calm everyone down, he added, "Take ten, and then we'll go back to rehearsing since we have a show on Friday."

The cast members had to tell the orchestra members who were still in the pit. Their heads had popped up, and the musicians were calling out, "What happened?"

Monica noticed the clarinet player shrugging his shoulders while looking at the drummer. Evidently they hadn't initiated this latest bit of chicanery.

Since Cap had placed his small surveillance cameras focused on all the dressing tables, he picked up the one which should have recorded the entire event. "I'll put this memory chip in my computer, and I hope it captured the whole thing," he said excitedly.

But in a few minutes, he returned and shook his head in a negative fashion. "Somehow an object got placed directly in front of the lens. We got zilch." Cap's crestfallen face reflected his disappointment.

When Milt heard the news no image of the ghost existed, he said, "I'm rather glad because I don't want to look at that horrible face again." Meredith put her arm around him as the two walked back toward the coffee and tea area.

Feeling the need for a little refreshment, Monica followed the two and put several coins in the vending machine for a diet Dr. Pepper.

Milt had recovered enough to sip a cup of tea which Hugh had handed him. The wounded tenor kept touching his head where he had bumped it. After several more swallows of tea, he proclaimed, "I'm not going to let this event interrupt the opera. *I will* sing. This demented witch, this evil spirit, will *not* destroy my art."

A couple of the chorus girls sitting at the table cooed, "You are so brave." Milt sighed when he heard this adulation. Meredith had wet several paper towels in cold water and dabbed at his forehead in a wifely fashion.

Monica, who believed he had just made up the ghost thing to get attention, decided to test his imagination. Because of her fake cold, she didn't get very close to him. She shouted across the table, "Did this spirit have on a long gown or was she just shrouded in mist? I've heard ghosts usually wear flowing robes, no hats, and no shoes."

Milt paused. "It happened so quickly. Yes, I believe she wore a long gown, but I couldn't see too well because of the swirling mist surrounding her. When she glared at me, her eyes burned like hot coals. It was terrible. I do remember those fiery eyes."

"One or two eyes?"

"Two eyes, for God's sake. She wasn't an odd looking alien or a creature from the Black Lagoon. She was just a woman in a gown with two blazing eyes."

"Was she a blonde or brunette? Short or long hair? Curly or straight?"

"Well, I didn't see her hair that well. I think it was dark. Long, but I can't remember if she had curls."

"What color was her dress? Did it have a high or low cut neck?" probed Monica.

"Good Lord, I can't remember all those details." Milt turned away from Monica and sipped his tea.

Monica left Milt with his groupies, grabbed Leslie by the elbow, and steered her to the dressing room. A large, flowery cosmetic bag sat on a shelf directly in front of the lens of the camera.

Monica said, "Since many people jostled one another in the room, it could have been inadvertently moved around. But I think Milt put this bag in front of the lens before he flattened himself on the floor. The big fake just wanted attention for the TV program."

Leslie added, "I think you're right. Did you notice when Cap came in with his camera, Milt made sure he turned his face toward the left. He told me once his left side is more photogenic. Frankly, I can't see any difference."

"He's not the only camera hog. Have you noticed how everybody dresses up for rehearsals?" commented Monica as they walked back to the refreshment area. Monica wanted to trip Milt up with his story, but for the moment didn't have a clue how to do it.

Monica noted every time she got fairly close to Milt, he scooted his chair back. On impulse she pretended to sneeze. He ran out of the refreshment area and back on stage.

Later, when Monica spoke to Leslie, she reprimanded herself, "I'm so pathetic. I've really set a new low to get a private laugh today."

Leslie said, "Keep sneezing, Monica. It's fun to watch Milt jump."

"I'm glad I'm not the only one who has sunk to that level," whispered Monica. "We need to watch Milt in the future, along with the drummer and the short clarinet player. I still want to find the original prankster, but it's harder with these new jokers getting into the act."

Monica glanced at the wall with the light switches where Joe was still on guard duty. He had pulled over a chair and was reading a newspaper. "Hey, Joe, How's it going?" she asked.

"I'm bored. I have a lot to do, but I'm stuck here," he complained.

"What do you think happened with Milt? Do you believe a womanly spirit pushed him?" asked Monica.

"Knocked down by a female mist? No way. But I'm not saying anything. I'm just going to do my job," he muttered.

"Cap's crew plans on staying here all night, but I doubt Miss Smog will return." Monica leaned against the wall and looked over the set of the final scene in front of the Colosseum. "Joe, you did a great job of designing the set for this opera."

"Yes, I love the theater, but I can't act very well. I was a theater major in college for a couple years. At first I wanted to be an actor, but it didn't work out. Set design was my next love. But you can't make much money unless you hit it big in LA or New York. So I switched to business. I'm now an accountant by day and a set designer and prop man at night."

He pushed back his chair and tilted it so he could recline a bit on the back two legs.

"Do you design the sets for many other theater companies?" asked Monica as she looked over the crowd to find Leslie.

"I do. I've done about six this year. I don't take on design work during tax season. That wouldn't work at all. But I like to be creative, and creativity isn't encouraged in the accounting world."

"You told me before you worked on the play, *Blithe Spirit*. What effects did you do?"

"During the seance scene, the dead return. They knock things off shelves, play music, and break stuff. I loved figuring out how to make the phonograph come on by itself, the lights go on and off, and voices coming from nowhere." Joe smiled as he remembered the fun of this past show.

"Really? You did all those things to resemble paranormal activity?" A light bulb blazed in Monica's brain as she contemplated Joe's accomplishments. Instead of searching for Leslie in the crowd, she turned and looked squarely at Joe with questioning eyes.

"Don't look at me that way," Joe protested. "No, no, I haven't pulled any of these tricks in this production. I'm not the phantom of the opera."

"I didn't think you were, but you could be a big help to Cap because you know how to fabricate voices and make other gimmicks. For instance, how do you make smoke? We all saw it the other night." Monica wondered why she hadn't pursued his know-how before.

"Sure, the easiest way of making mist or smoke is to use dry ice. But, I'm not talking to Cap. Hugh is pushing the phantom of the opera thing because it's good for business, so I just do my job, but guarding the light switch is a big bore."

Joe yawned to emphasize his position. "The only bit of amusement tonight was Milt's saying he had been pushed over by a female mist." Remembering the incident brought out a couple chuckles.

Monica added, "I thought it was a good one too. Miss Smog knocking down a 200 pound man is a whopper."

"But there's no business like show business," Joe said. Monica nodded in agreement and was about to ask him another question when Nick appeared holding one of the large imitation palm leaves used in the tavern scene.

Nick walked over to Joe and said, "I'll take over for awhile so you can have a break. I can sew this rip while I'm guarding the lights."

"Thanks a lot. I need one," answered Joe who stood up, stretched, and walked off. "See you later." His lanky figure ambled off toward the work area in the back.

Monica asked Nick, "What did you think about Miss Smog?"

He grinned and said, "That's a good name for the misty spook. She packs quite a wallop."

Nick changed the subject and started complaining. "That TV crew is making it hard for us to work on the set. They're all over the place, pushing our stuff around, throwing hamburger wrappers on the floor, leaving cans of soda everywhere. I hope they leave soon."

"I imagine they'll stay for awhile," commented Monica.

"Yeah, I suppose so. You know, I started thinking about something I saw the night of the murder. It could have been nothing, but then it might be important. I saw. . ."

Nick stopped in the middle of his sentence when Hugh announced on the microphone, "All cast members on stage, please."

Monica said, "I have to go now, but I'm interested in what you saw. I'll find you after rehearsal, and we can talk then."

"Sure, if I'm not on this chair, I'll be in the back working on these palm leaves that keep tearing," said Nick.

"See you later," called out Monica as she headed for the stage. When she took her place in the chorus of gypsies, she wondered what he could have seen. Maybe it would lead to a break in the case.

9

Rick went to Monica's room at Four Hills High School after the bell had rung to dismiss the students for the day. "Whew, those kids can really move fast," he commented to her as he walked in the door. "Now I know how the salmon feel when they're moving upstream against the flow."

Rick sat down in one of the student desks. His long legs bumped against the writing arm of the chair.

"It's worse in the parking lot when they're behind steering wheels," added Monica as she put a paper clip on a stack of papers. "Before I go, I need to erase my boards." She slid an eraser over the notes she had written on *Henry V.*

"My classes went really well today. The kids like Henry because he was boisterous, irresponsible, and daring as a young prince. When he became king, he changed. He took his duties seriously and left his wild life behind. I think the kids secretly hope they can do the same."

A disheveled boy darted into the room and handed Monica his essay. "I forgot to turn in my paper," he mumbled before he sprinted out the door. Monica added his work to her stack, repositioned the paper clip, and put the pile of essays in her tote.

"I have about four hours of grading ahead of me," sighed Monica as she eyed her fat tote. "And I won't be able to put in more than an hour or so tonight because of the rehearsal. And speaking of rehearsals, I told you about Miss Smog last night, but I forgot to tell you about Nick."

"Is it as funny as Milt and Miss Smog?" asked Rick who started to smile as he thought about last night's incident.

"No, it isn't funny at all. Nick told me he saw something that might be important. Just when he opened his mouth to reveal what it was, Hugh called us on stage. I looked for him after we rehearsed and couldn't find him. Maybe tonight he'll tell me," said Monica as she set down the dusty eraser, turned off her computer, and shoved back a student chair that had gotten out of line.

"I'm ready," she said.

"What will it be today? Chocolate cake? Cherry pie? Ice cream sundae?" he asked.

Monica wiggled her nose as she contemplated various goodies. "Hot fudge sundae," she answered. They walked to his car in the now empty parking lot and headed for Baskin Robbins.

After polishing off a hot fudge sundae with whipped cream, peanuts, and a cherry on top, Monica nixed dinner. "I probably ate 2000 calories, but it was yummy," she confessed to Rick who had stuck with a meager one dip sorbet.

"I have just enough time to run home, feed the cats and dog, and change into my jeans before going to the theater," she added.

"Let me know if Nick tells you anything important," said Rick as he scrunched his paper napkin into the empty dish. "On the other hand, let me know if what he says isn't important. I like to hear from you," he said with a wink. A lock of black hair fell over his forehead. Each time it happened, Monica's heart got all squishy.

Monica blushed slightly. "Sure, I'll call you."

When Monica and Leslie arrived at the theater, they saw five police cars, yellow tape everywhere, TV news crews, and lots of rubbernecks. "What happened?" they said in unison as they stood near the yellow tape on the sidewalk.

"Murder. A body was found in there," said one of the onlookers who pointed to the theater.

"Oh my God! Who was it?" asked Monica as she shuddered and felt little prickles of fear running up her backbone. Leslie sucked in her breath and grabbed Monica's arm.

"I don't know who, but I heard it was a man," said one of the people standing close by. Another jostled over and hissed, "It's the evil spirit."

A male voice bellowed out, "What happened?"

A TV news reporter who was packing up his equipment answered, "Listen to the 10 o'clock news. You'll hear all about it."

An ambulance pulled away from the curb and took off silently. Monica followed it with her eyes as did the others. After this sobering moment, people began to disperse in all directions. The show was over.

Monica and Leslie swivelled their heads in an attempt to find other cast members while they stood outside the yellow tape. Monica didn't see anyone from the production, but she recognized Rick, talking with a uniformed police officer. "Detective Miller," she called out.

Rick turned towards her voice, saw her with Leslie, and walked over. "Bad news. Joe came in about 5:00 p.m. and found Nick lying on the stage with a dagger in his back." He shook his head and added, "I thought all the weird stuff at the theater was just horseplay done by some kid who wanted to have a little fun by scaring the adults. Now we have a real crime, murder."

"Murder, most foul," mumbled Monica.

Leslie sucked in her breath and shuddered. "I can't believe it. I didn't really know him because he was always hammering or painting in the back."

"I just talked to him last night," said Monica while she tried to digest the awful news. "He was going to tell me what he saw that might have a bearing on the case. Hugh called for the cast to go on stage so Nick said he would tell me later. My God, it happened just like in so many of the mysteries I've read."

"What do you mean?" asked Leslie.

"A character says he knows who the murderer is, and just at that moment he's shot through the heart. Or just as a dying murdered person tries to write the name of his killer in blood on the floor, he croaks before he can scrawl the first letter. It happens all the time in books but not in real life. Life imitates art. I can't believe it," Monica babbled.

"Do you remember if anyone could have over-heard you when that conversation took place last night?" asked Rick.

"I'll have to think for a minute." Monica went through the scene and recited it to Rick. "Nick had just relieved Joe on the light switch duty, and I went over to chat with him. He leaned his chair against the wall on its two back legs while I faced him. We chatted while people were milling around behind us. Once I felt a little jostle from someone behind me, but I didn't turn to see who it was."

"Was Nick glancing around while he spoke to you, or did he look at you squarely in the eyes?" asked Rick.

"What an intriguing idea. If I could only remember." Monica chewed her lower lip and wrinkled her forehead. "Maybe he moved his eyes back and forth a bit. Yes, he definitely did. Not in an exaggerated way, like moving his whole body to see if someone was listening, but just a couple flickers."

"It could mean something or nothing," said Rick. "I saw Hugh about 30 minutes ago and told him to call off the rehearsal. There's a sign on the stage door. We'll take off the tape tomorrow so the cast can come back. Don't worry. The show will be able to open on Friday night as scheduled."

"Could I just go inside for a little peek? I wouldn't get in the way," pleaded Monica who longed to solve the crime or at least contribute meaningful insights.

Rick lowered his voice and spoke in a conspiratorial way, "I can't let you in right now because the tech guys are working, but if you come back in a couple hours, it'll be okay. In the meantime would you help me out?"

"Sure," whispered Monica, "I'll be glad to do whatever you want." Monica loved sleuthing as much as she loved Shakespeare.

"We found out Nick worked in a bowling alley during the day, but the last couple months, he's been helping Monty Malone, a fellow who gives lectures on how to make money. He gives a lecture five nights a week at an empty store in a strip mall. I couldn't get him by phone to tell him about the death of his employee, but if you would go over there and give him the bad news, it would help me out."

"Sure," said Monica quickly.

"You might ask Mr. Malone about Nick's friends." Rick grinned at her because he knew she wanted to help investigate.

"Where is this strip mall, and when does he start his lecture?" asked Monica who acted like a dog ready to catch the ball.

"The strip mall is at Fourth St. near Menaul Blvd. You can't miss the place since the sign says, 'Monty Malone, the Money Man' in huge letters. His lectures start at 7:00 p.m. so you have about 30 minutes before he goes into his spiel. I've heard he's quite a salesman," added Rick who signaled another member of the police force with his eyes while he gave a good-bye wave to Monica.

Monica jingled her keys and said, "Come on, Leslie, let's go." They both trotted over to the car, jumped in, and buckled their seat belts. Monica made good time as she managed to hit a number of green lights.

The huge sign in green neon pulsed, sparkled, and dominated the little mall. Monica parked directly in front of the store which didn't bode well for the size of Monty's audience.

When they entered the place, Monty Malone in a green suit bustled over to them, extended his hand, and said, "Hi, folks, I'm the Money Man. I'm here to tell you how you can be a millionaire."

Monica noticed a $100 bill sticking out of his jacket handkerchief pocket and two $100 bills sticking out of each of his pants pockets. Monty's chubby body, encased in a suit too small, bulged out over his shirt collar and over his belt buckle.

Folding chairs faced the back wall where a large plastic tree dominated a small platform. On the branches were hung $10, $20, and $50 bills, like leaves. Monica wondered how people could resist the urge to pick money off the tree. A microphone and a small table piled with books completed the objects on the platform.

Monica's eyes roved from the money on the tree to the money on Monty. After recovering from the brief green shock, she shook his hand and said, "How do you do, Mr. Malone. I'm Monica Walters, and this is my friend, Leslie Dunhill. I'm here to bring sad news about your employee, Nick Johnson."

Leslie greeted him and shook his hand.

Monty Malone's expansive, blustery manner disappeared. "What happened?" he asked. "I didn't expect him tonight since he's working at the opera, but he helps me out when he can."

"I've been asked by the Police Department to give you the news. Nick is dead. He's been murdered," blurted out Monica.

"Murdered? That guy was murdered? I can't believe it!" Monty sat down in one of the wobbly folding chairs. "How did it happen?"

"I really don't know all the details because the police are pretty mum, but his body was discovered about 5:00 tonight on the stage at the Kimo Theater. He was stabbed in the chest," explained Monica. "You'll be able to find out more on the 10 o'clock news."

"I liked the guy. He wasn't a talker, so I really didn't know much about him." Monty paused and tugged at his collar. "He told me he wanted to be a millionaire. He really wanted a fancy car, a Ferrari, and a big house with a swimming pool on Rio Grande Blvd. A lot of people want expensive cars and fancy houses."

Monica replied, "The American dream. That's what Gatsby wanted. I'm a teacher and my students read Scott Fitzgerald's book *The Great Gatsby*."

"Never read it, but I missed a lot of classes when I went to school," confessed Monty.

"Do you know the names of any of Nick's friends? I'd like to tell them before they hear it on the news." Monica turned one of the folding chairs around so she could face Monty. After she sat down on the rickety chair, she took a notebook out of her enormous tote. Leslie sat next to her.

"Do you mind waiting a bit? People are coming in, and I have to start my lecture." Monty jumped up to greet a couple of young men and bellowed out, "Hi, folks, I'm the Money Man. Come on in, and I'll tell you how to be a millionaire."

At 7:00 Monty stood on the platform and began his spiel to the nine members of the audience. "If you do what I say, you're going to be driving a Mercedes, wearing a mink coat, and swimming in your own Olympic pool. You can eat lobster and steak every night, fly in your own jet to Hawaii, and sit at the 10 yard line at the Super Bowl."

The eyes of the members of the audience glistened.

"Did he refer to buying a mink coat? Fur coats are out. I'd be the first one to throw catsup on a woman who dared to wear a mink coat," huffed Monica.

"Indeed, I'd spit on the coat first," Leslie said as indignant as Monica.

Monty continued with the golden possibilities that money could buy. "You can play golf at St.

Andrews in Scotland, drink champagne in Paris, ski in Switzerland, live in a mansion on five acres of land, and employ a bunch of servants."

Two members of the audience licked their lips.

"Now, folks, the fastest way to get money is to rob a bank, not a convenience store, but a bank. Have your wheel man waiting outside the door, drive down the street, stop at a parking lot, switch cars, and go to the airport. You can be on your way to the French Riviera before the cops get moving."

Monica and Leslie, along with the rest of the audience looked stunned.

Monty smiled. "It might be the fastest way to get money, but it's illegal. That was my little joke, folks." Monty paused while the audience recovered and laughed nervously. "Another fast way to get money is to marry the boss's daughter. That, my friends, is legal, but it's not easy to do. Lots of bosses don't have good looking, unmarried daughters." Monty chuckled and the audience did too.

"When you talk about stocks and bonds, there is a simple answer. Buy low and sell high. You can't miss."

Monty tugged at his tie, lowered the knot, and unbuttoned his collar. He removed his suit jacket and rolled up his sleeves. Monica thought by doing this, he indicated to the audience he was now getting down to business.

"Here in my book I've written down the methods you can use to make your millions. No joking now, folks. It's all written down in plain English." Monty continued his spiel, "In my book you'll find legal, easy methods of getting money." Without saying what the methods were, he talked on for the next 20 minutes.

"This book sells for just $29.00, but as a special deal, just for today, you can buy it for only $14.95. Tomorrow it'll be $29, but tonight you get a real bargain." Monty whipped out a book from a big box at his side. The long title in bright green letters was *You Can be a Millionaire. It's as Easy as Picking Money off a Tree."*

At that moment he went over to his plastic tree and pulled off a $20 bill. Everyone laughed. He took more bills from the tree, spread them out a little, and used the money as a fan to cool off his face. More laughter.

Monica gasped in surprise when five people lined up and shelled out $14.95 for the book. "Leslie, can you believe it? All those people are buying dreams, blue sky, hope. It's really very sad."

"Nothing we can do about it," muttered Leslie.

Clutching their books, the people filed out of the store front. Monty came back and sat down with Monica and Leslie. He commented, "Small crowd, but they bought. Some nights I've had 100 or so people, sitting and standing in the back. Nick really helped by getting out the books and taking in the money. Nice guy, I'll miss him."

"Have you thought of any of his friends or family now that you've had more time to think about it?" asked Monica who hoped he could come up with some sort of lead. She leaned forward and looked at him as though her gaze could help bring out information.

"No, he didn't talk about family. He mentioned a girlfriend occasionally. He said she would sure like to go to Paris and see all the art in the Louvre. Just a while ago he mentioned I'd helped him, and maybe he and his girl could go to Europe." Monty paused. "I thought it was odd because he never bought a copy of my book."

"If you think of anything that might be relevant, please call the police and ask for Detective Miller," said Monica as she stood up to leave. "By the way, does anyone ever try to steal money from your tree?"

"Don't tell, but it's fake. Looks like the real thing until you scrutinize it. I made it myself," boasted Monty. He smiled and continued with the joke, "Making your own is another quick way of becoming a millionaire."

Monica became intrigued and walked over to the tree. She studied a $20 bill on both sides but couldn't find a flaw. "This is a good forgery."

"Thank you," he said with pride in his voice.

"You don't ever try to pass one off, do you?" teased Monica in a jocular way.

"Only at church," he quipped. He stuck out his index finger so it looked like a gun and said, "Gottcha."

Monty pulled a couple sodas out of a cooler and offered them to Monica and Leslie. Both refused, but he popped the tab on one and took a long drink. Monica put her empty notebook back in her tote, waved farewell to Monty, and walked to her car.

After driving Leslie home, Monica hoped Rick would let her into the theater so she could snoop. She would tell him what she found out. The most intriguing question was how Nick planned to acquire enough money to take his girlfriend to Paris by working at a bowling alley.

10

Monica returned to the theater as soon as she dropped off Leslie. The crime scene tape still covered a portion of the sidewalk in front of the stage door, but she ignored it and slipped under.

When she opened the door, no one yelled at her so she kept on moving to the stage. Rick was leaning against a wall of the Colosseum and pointing at one of Cap's cameras. Another policeman was removing it from its position.

As soon as Rick saw Monica standing on the corner of the stage, he gestured for her to come over. "Hi, how did it go with Monty Malone?"

"He said he didn't know any of Nick's friends, but he talked about a girl. By the way, have you ever seen Monty's money tree? He has fake bills instead of leaves which he picks off to emphasize how easy it is to make money. It's a great visual." Monica gazed into Rick's eyes as she related her little scrap of news.

"I've heard he's quite a showman. I'd like to see that tree myself," replied Rick. "I'll have to talk to him soon. No one seems to know much about Nick. Even Joe, who works with him on the set for the opera, knows very little. Joe said Nick skulked around quietly and often came in early or stayed late. He even may have slept here because we found a sleeping bag in the back behind a piece of scenery."

Rick's stomach growled. While he soothed it with his hand, he said, "I'm really hungry. Do you want to get a bite to eat after I finish a few things here?" he asked.

"Sure, I'm hungry myself. I'll just sort of look around while I wait. I won't touch anything," she promised.

"I didn't think you would. I won't be long." Rick walked over to look at the camera that several men were dismantling. The taller one shook his head and poured broken parts into a sack.

As Monica thought about the broken camera, she wondered if the murderer had wacked it before or after the crime. Was the timing important? After dismissing that thought, she concentrated on the little cozy nook where the police had found the sleeping bag.

In the far back, a number of large, long panels leaned against a wall. She noted the panels rested on a contraption which held them in place, preventing them from collapsing. Between the wall and the slanting panels, a triangular cubby was visible; however, if the sleeping bag was stuffed back about three feet, no one would ever see it.

Monica crouched down on her hands and knees in order to crawl into the space. She didn't feel any dust bunnies, just smooth floor. The area allowed enough room for a person to be comfy and cozy.

To get out, Monica had to crawl backwards. As she was manipulating this awkward motion, her hand bumped the side of one of the panels. She felt a jagged edge of paper. When she tugged, it came out. Once into the light, she realized she had grabbed a corner of a photograph.

She stared at the fragment which showed a man's arm with his hand snaked around a woman's waist. No heads, no legs, just human middles. Dark clothing for both didn't reveal a style or age. Could this arm belong to Rob?

Monica rushed over to Rick and handed him the scrap. "Look what I found while I was crawling around in that little sleeping space," she announced with a tinge of pride.

He scrutinized the fragment, put it in a plastic bag, and mumbled, "Probably means nothing, but we'll take a closer look later."

"Hey, Rick. Cap is here," called one of the policemen.

Rick perked up when he heard his name and turned to face the stage door.

When Cap strode in, he asked, "What happened?"

"I'm sorry to tell you this, but an intruder came in and destroyed some of your cameras."

Cap saw the plastic sack with all the broken parts. He erupted with a loud, "Shit!" Quicky, he looked around the walls where he had placed other cameras to catch the ghost. As he tracked down each one, he barked, "Shit." He grabbed his baseball hat off his head and threw it on the floor. "Do you know how much those cameras cost?" he bellowed.

Rick ignored the rhetorical question. "Let's check the ones in back." Both men hurried to the area where the scenery was stored.

While Cap had been taking stock of each of his cameras on stage, Monica had followed with her eyes. She realized some were hidden from view very cleverly. How could the murderer find each one? Unless of course, he already knew where they were.

"Every last one! Ruined. Shit! Shit! Shit!" Cap thundered as he returned from his tour of his equipment. "I'll have to order more from New York. It'll take days. I might miss the spook." Cap sat down on a folding chair, bent over slightly, and put his head in his hands.

Rick offered him a can of diet Dr. Pepper. At first he shook his head but a second later reached out for the soda.

Monica tried to put a good spin on Cap's fear of missing a ghostly appearance. "Maybe the spook won't come for awhile because of all the police commotion that's going on here."

"Huh? Spooks aren't scared by the police. They do their own thing whenever they wish." He took out his cell phone and poked in a number before he walked away to have his private conversation.

Monica tilted her head towards Rick. "What do you think the killer used to bash in the cameras?"

"We found a 12 foot board with particles of glass in one end," answered Rick. "Lots of boards back there. No trouble for him to find one. He brought his own weapon, however. It was a regular butcher knife, not a modified stage dagger." Rick stroked his chin which bristled with new growth.

"Do you think there's any connection between this murder and the other one?" Monica asked Rick as she put her hands in her jean pockets. Before Rick could answer, he was summoned by a member of his homicide team.

"Hey, Rick, there's a guy who wants to talk to you. He's wearing a green suit with a $50 bill sticking out of a pocket," shouted a policeman.

"It's got to be Monty. Maybe he thought of something," said Monica as she turned around to face the stage door.

"I'm never going to get out of here. Would you mind if we just had a bite at the cast table over there?" asked Rick.

She smiled at him and said, "Sure, that's fine."

He gave $20 to a cop near him. "Buy a couple burgers, fries, and chocolate shakes." He looked at Monica and asked, " Okay with you? I know you like chocolate shakes."

"Sounds good," she replied. She never turned down good fast food. Luckily her genetic metabolism allowed her to eat fattening foods and not gain weight.

Rick raised his arm and beckoned Monty to come over. All the cops stopped whatever they were doing to take a gander at the green suited man with money sticking out of his pockets. He bounced across the stage, held his arm out for a handshake, and exclaimed, "Hi, I'm Monty Malone."

He pumped Rick's hand so vigorously that a $10 bill dropped to the floor. He picked it up, waved it in the air, and exclaimed, "I'm the money man."

One of the cops called out, "Do you give away any samples?"

Monty in a good-natured way, shouted back, "No, but if you come to my lecture, you can see my money tree. Buy my book, and you'll find out how to make a million."

Rick gestured for Monty to sit down on a folding chair over on the side of the stage. Rick pulled up a chair and faced him. Monica felt it would be presumptuous to sit with them so she moved over to the dingy table used by the cast. She made sure she plopped down on the closest chair to the two men so she could eavesdrop.

When Monty sat down, his belly hung down over his pants. He started out in his brazen fashion. "I just thought I'd come down and tell you what I know. Nick was a quiet fellow, but we talked a bit before my lectures. He really wanted a nice car, a Ferrari. Used to show me pictures of them."

Rick took out his notebook and pen.

Monty continued, "Well, tonight I got to thinking. Nick said something funny just the other night. I always start my lectures with a joke that bank robbery is a fast way of getting a lot of money. It warms up the audience, you know. Nick said I should use blackmail instead of bank robbery. He said besides being fast, the money keeps on coming. Then he laughed and laughed. Sort of odd, I thought."

"Do you think he was blackmailing someone?" asked Rick whose eyes sharpened as he looked up from his notebook.

"I don't know, but he just kept laughing. You know, he looked kind of chipper, like a cat that swallowed a canary." Monty paused. "He was just like a cat in other ways. He walked quietly. I'd see him here, and before I knew it, he'd be somewhere else." Monty leaned back in his chair and tugged at the knot in his tie.

"Do you have any idea where he went on his time off?"

"He didn't have much time off. He worked at the bowling alley during the afternoons, at the opera set four nights a week, and at my place two nights. Weekends are my big nights. He'd help by bringing out my books and selling them. Every now and then he'd sweep the floor. He might have taken a few twenties off my tree. I noticed it looked a little barren a week or so ago."

After Monty had reported on his depleted tree, he furrowed his brow. "I wonder if he tried to pass some of my phony money?"

"I haven't heard of any merchants reporting forged bills to the police," commented Rick. "I'm interested in the suggestion of blackmail. Nick worked on the set of *Blithe Spirit*. Perhaps he heard or saw something connected to that murder."

Since the two men didn't seem to pay any attention to her, Monica slowly scooted over towards them so she wouldn't miss a word.

"We need to find out what Nick saw, heard, or found. Not going to be easy," Rick tipped his chair back on two legs, balanced it precariously, and stroked his bristly chin again

Monty kept gnawing his lower lip as if this nibbling would increase his recall. "Might as well go home. I can't think of anything more," mumbled Monty. He stood up and held out his hand for another shake.

"Thanks for coming in," said Rick. "Keep in touch. Here's my card." Monty left slowly with his head down as if in deep thought.

A few minutes later, the wonderful smell of hamburgers, onions, and fries wafted through the air. As soon as the police officer set down the sacks of food on the marred wooden table, Monica and Rick quickly ripped the paper, shook out the salty fries on a napkin, and unwrapped their burgers.

Monica had just taken a big bite when one of the policemen called out, "Hey, Rick, you have another visitor."

Belinda rushed over to Rick. "What happened? Hugh didn't really explain when he called. I just heard that little man who worked in the back is dead. What was his name? I know this scare will affect my voice. I can feel my throat tighten."

Belinda massaged her throat in an attempt to relax her vocal cords. She opened and closed her mouth a couple times and belted out a couple arpeggios.

It seemed to Monica the singers constantly vocalized arpeggios during conversations. At first, it seemed odd, but now she was used to these musical trills which reminded her of larks warbling in the morning sunshine.

When Belinda's operatic voice resounded throughout the theater, all other sounds of work and conversation stopped. She looked around with a pleased smile and murmured, "I still have it."

Rick graciously said, "Yes, ma'am, you have a beautiful voice."

"I'm very delicate, you know. This murder could blemish my performance. Just thinking about that poor little man and the blood on stage could affect my voice. I hope you will clear this mess up by opening night."

Belinda shook her hair which floated around her neck and settled in an attractive curl over her shoulder. She buttoned up her jacket as if she were about to leave.

While Monica finished chewing a bite of her hamburger, she had a thought. She turned to Rick who had just dipped a french fry in a dab of catsup and said, "Belinda just brought up a point. What about the blood stains on the boards? It will be impossible to redo the floor by this weekend."

Rick popped the potato chunk in his mouth. "A rug will cover it. Hugh will have to find a rug to cover the spot."

"A rug? A rug doesn't fit in the plaza in front of the Colosseum. It can't be a rug. I don't like rugs," insisted Belinda.

"Maybe it'll affect her voice," snickered one of the young cops in a low voice to his friend as they were dusting fingerprint powder on the long board.

"I heard that," snapped Belinda as she sent him a frosty look. "People just don't understand artists," she said for everyone's benefit. "We artists are sensitive to our environments. Ordinary people see the world much as cows do." From the back came a soft mooing sound and muffled guffaws.

"That's not funny," said Belinda.

More mooing erupted followed by a shushing sound.

To keep Belinda's mind from the mooing, Monica decided to reassure her. Using her soft voice, Monica said, "You have a gorgeous voice. After a good night's sleep, you'll feel better. Let Hugh worry about the spot on the stage floor. He'll take care of it. He might be able to get someone to sand it or whatever."

Monica's words soothed Belinda who sighed and sat down. Rick kept popping catsup topped french fries in his mouth but said nothing. Monica, too, loved catsup and split another little packet for her fries while she bit into the hamburger. As the juicy hamburger oozed a bit, Monica licked it off her lip.

Abruptly Belinda jumped up, waved good-bye, and left. Monica grinned at Rick. "I almost laughed when the mooing started, but I held it in."

Rick's eyes danced as he confessed, "I almost choked on my hamburger. I probably should reprimand the boys, but it was funny." Rick swiped across his mouth with his paper napkin. "That tasted good. Now, I'm ready for a couple more hours of work."

Monica sighed. "I have at least an hour of grading to do before I can hit the sack. I'd better head off for home."

Rick leaned across the table, touched her hand, and whispered, "Thanks for coming. Your visit was the best part of the day." They goo-goo eyed each other for a long time before Monica got up and went home.

11

The next day Monica kept thinking about Nick's murder. Since he had been a quiet man, no one seemed to know much about him. He had worked with both Joe and Monty, yet they didn't provide any real leads although Monica felt Monty knew more because of the implied blackmail.

While the students were writing a paragraph, Monica tried to grade a few tests, but her thoughts kept returning to Monty. She needed to grill him, in a nice way, of course. After school was over, she'd make a little trip to the store with the money tree.

The door to Monty's place was open when she arrived. She walked in and saw Monty drinking coffee while he slouched over his little table. He didn't get up when he saw her but merely waved his hand in a half-hearted greeting.

Monica called out, "How's it going, Monty?"

Monty lifted his head and said, "Not so good."

"What happened?"

"My life sucks. I've lost my gusto. I don't have much money. I can't even pay my rent for next month," he moaned.

"But you said sometimes you've had over 100 people at your lectures," Monica replied as she sat down in a folding chair across from him.

"I lied. The most I've had is 15. Sometimes I sell some books, but often times there's someone in the audience who asks *the question*."

"What's *the question*?" asked Monica as she wrinkled her forehead.

"Why aren't you a millionaire? No one buys a book after that. The kids these days are thinking rather than dreaming. I need dreamers, people who buy hope."

Monica couldn't argue with that. "When I was here, I thought about *the question*, but I was too polite to ask."

"What is happening to these kids? Why aren't they nice and polite like you? Now they think and speak up." Monty took another sip of coffee.

After his statement about her politeness, she hesitated before she asked a question about his book. "I'm curious about the examples you use in your book. Would you mind telling me?"

"The examples are things like winning the lottery, finding oil on your land, locating a treasure left by a pirate. Stuff like that. Highly unlikely, but possible. Nothing illegal like I joked about when I was warming up the audience," explained Monty. "I've tried out some of my ideas, but none of them have worked. I'm a loser."

"Well, isn't there something you've always wanted to do?" prompted Monica.

"Yes, I've had my own dream. It's probably too late to follow it."

"It's never too late." Monica wanted to encourage him.

"But I'm 35. Could I still reach for the stars?"

"Yes, don't let your age stop you. The middle thirties are a time for getting what you want out of life," urged Monica.

"Maybe, I still could." Monty's eyes started to glisten.

"What do you want to do?"

" I want to be a pimp."

"What? Did I hear right?" squeaked Monica.

"Pimp, I want to be a pimp," he repeated.

"For God's sake, why?" Monica stared at the slumped figure of the once brassy money man who had just revealed his dream.

"I'd be in show business. It would be easy. I'd rent or buy a motel, sit at the desk, and take the money from the johns as they went up to the rooms. It would be a night job, but I could live with that. If any person thought it was a regular motel, that would be okay too. I could watch television while sitting at my desk. Piece of cake." Monty brightened a bit as he thought about the ease and tranquility of being a pimp.

"Prostitution is illegal," Monica replied. Scads of disadvantages came to her mind. She connected pimps with gangsters in black suits with guns in their pockets. She'd heard they beat their girls, took all their money, and plied them with drugs. They had names like Scarface, Mr. Big, and Bugsy. The Chamber of Commerce didn't recognize the business.

"I'd tell the girls to be discreet. The johns would never tell. They don't want their wives to know. Most cops sort of look the other way, don't you think. It's not a real crime because the girls get paid."

"It may not seem like a crime to you, but it's illegal."

Monty continued, "I'd interview the girls first. I'd give them the regular 40 hour week, 9 to 5 but at night, of course. I haven't decided about the rate per encounter or trick. I'm not sure of the correct term for you-know-what. Doesn't that sound reasonable?" Monty sat up as he contemplated the working conditions he had formulated for his enterprise.

"Prostitution isn't an average business. You're exploiting women," snapped Monica. "You'd be making money off the misery of women who have already been abused by the world." Monica didn't know any prostitutes herself, but she had read about the terrible lives of young girls forced into selling their bodies.

"Oh, I'd ask them before I hired them if they really wanted to go into this line of work. I wouldn't hire young girls either. I have my standards," replied Monty. "For an entry-level hooker or *ho*, the girl would need to be at least 18."

"Would there be a different pay scale for girls who had a couple years of experience?" asked Monica.

"Yes, experienced girls would make more money. I've also decided to provide sodas, doughnuts, and other snacks during working hours. Each girl could have her own TV, and I'd order a number of magazine subscriptions to provide entertainment on slow nights."

"I'm glad you're trying to make a good work environment for the girls. But instead of chocolate chip cookies and *People* magazine, they might take heroin or meth during their breaks," said Monica.

"If other things were available, they might not take drugs. Besides sweets, I'd have healthy food like apples and bananas," said Monty who appeared to want to make life pleasant for his employees.

"There are some dangers involved," cautioned Monica. "Other pimps might barge in with guns. Fights could break out between the johns. Drug dealers might use your lobby as a place for selling their stuff. Often crime is involved with prostitution."

"What a killjoy you've turned out to be. You're raining on my parade," whined Monty who slumped down further in his chair.

Monica realized she might as well stop talking about Monty's dream so she just threw out a final caution. "I hope you think this business over before you get involved."

"Right now I have to pay the rent. I might take a day job for awhile. I sold shoes for a couple months last year. Selling shoes to men is great, but women are terrible. Once I took out eight pairs of shoes for a lady who couldn't make up her mind. After half an hour of my time, she left without buying a single pair."

Frustrated by this conversation, Monica stood up, jingled the keys in her pocket, and glanced at her watch. "Did Nick, by the way, leave any of his stuff here?"

"He left a couple boxes in the back room. He said he didn't have much room in his apartment."

"Did you tell the police?" asked Monica.

"They never asked. They wanted names of his friends, girlfriend, and acquaintances. I don't know any names. He talked about a girl, but he didn't even give her a nickname like Babe or Cupcake. Like I said before, he didn't talk much about his personal life."

"Could you show me the boxes?"

"Sure, I don't want them." Monty lead Monica into a back room where boxes of his books on making easy money were stacked four high and four across the floor.

In a corner on the other side, Monty pointed to a couple shoe boxes. "Those are his. Take them with you and give them to the police or whatever. I may be living in this room if I don't pay the rent on my apartment," groused Monty who picked up the two boxes and handed them to Monica.

Monty kept prodding other containers. He tipped over a large paper sack that spilled out a pair of hiking boots which he kicked to the side. "I thought he left a couple more boxes, but I don't see them." Monty poked away at a pile of Christmas decorations, a blanket in plastic zip bag, and a stack of paperback mystery novels.

Monica rested the two boxes on her arm and said, "I'll give these to the police. If you find anything more, call Detective Rick Miller." She hurried out of the building and headed for the theater.

Because of the murder, Hugh was holding the tech and the dress rehearsal at the same time. The theater would be dark on Thursday so everyone would be rested and in good voice for opening night on Friday.

Monica felt the tension as soon as she entered through the stage door. High-pitched nervous laughter, purposeless frantic movement, and snatches of arias filled the theater. Monica thought there's no business like show business. The show would go on despite murder, most foul.

As she hurried to the dressing room for makeup, she saw Leslie. Monica couldn't wait to tell her news to her best friend. "I stopped in to see Monty before coming over. He gave me two shoe boxes of Nick's stuff. I'm dying to open them, but I don't want to be accused of tampering with the evidence. I called Rick, and he's coming over to get them."

"I'm pleased to hear you're showing some restrain. I thought you'd peek as soon as you put them in the car," bantered Leslie.

"As a matter of fact, when I set them down on the front seat, one of the lids sort of slid off, and I saw photographs and letters. I didn't ruffle through them but immediately put the lid back on," swore Monica as she put up her hand in the oath taking position.

"Lids don't stay on well these days. They're always sliding off," teased Leslie. Before they went into the dressing room, they bumped into various members of the cast who bustled around getting their costumes, makeup, and wigs.

Wearing his gladiator costume, Burt Brown strutted over to them and asked, "Is my wig on straight? I think my pigtail is off center."

Both women gazed at the back of his head and carefully judged the little black pigtail. "It's dead centered," said Monica.

Leslie nodded in agreement. "I didn't think gladiators wore pigtails."

"I wanted to wear the pigtail wig like the toreadors do, and Hugh okayed it. After all, the JC Sandal Co. doesn't fit in B.C. Rome either."

"Historians might be a little bothered by the liberties taken, but most people won't care," said Monica.

Burt fussed with the drape in his costume. "What about the color? Do you think it's too red? I wanted a more subdued scarlet shade to go better with my complexion."

Monica gushed, "You look great! That red hue blends beautifully with your complexion. You are the perfect, handsome gladiator or B.C. toreador."

Burt smiled, lifted his chin, and murmured, "Thank you, my dear." Evidently satisfied with what he was wearing, he started humming a couple bars from his opening number. He switched to running through a couple scales. "The air in here is stuffy. It's affecting my voice," he complained.

Monica scurried away from him and whispered to Leslie, "Injuries from improbable falls, quality of the air, blood diseases, loud furniture moving, and silly fortune-tellers seem to affect the voices of the singers. He's one of the worst."

Leslie agreed. Both women entered the dressing room where theater majors from the University were applying makeup. Five students smeared grease paint, mascara, and other enhancing products on five faces of the opera company.

Monica and Leslie sat down as soon as two seats were vacated. A young girl bent over Monica, pushed her hair away from her face, and secured the area by using a strip of paper to prevent tiny tendrils of hair from interfering with the makeup.

As the student started her work, Monica asked, "Have you been doing this for very long?"

"I'm taking a class right now, and helping out at this opera is the first real show I've done. Our professor is coming to check on us and give us a grade so I hope I get an A." The girl bubbled over with enthusiasm.

Monica automatically went into her teacher mode. "You're doing very well. I saw the excellent work you did on your last face."

Rick popped his head in the dressing room and waved at Monica. "Hi, you're looking good."

"Hi Rick," she said as she gave him a little smile. "I should be finished in a few minutes. I'll get those boxes out of my car." Monica couldn't move because at that moment the University student was outlining her eyes in a dark brown.

Rick called back, "Fine. I'll be checking out a couple things on the stage."

After he left, the girl asked, "Is he your boyfriend? Your eyes kind of glittered when he came in," she added.

Monica blushed and didn't know how to answer. "Well, sort of. I mean we're very good friends. Just good friends," she stammered.

When Monica looked in the mirror with her new face and black wig, she felt like a different person, which gave her a heady freedom. As she analyzed her transformation, she understood the intoxication of being in a show, even if she only had a very minor role. She almost skipped over to Rick who was standing in a corner of the stage.

"You look lovely," he said.

"I feel excited. I hope everything goes well. The cast has worked so hard to put on a good show," she commented as she patted her wig in the back. It felt a little odd to have all this new hair on her head.

"Break a leg," said Rick. "But I need to get to work. Where are the boxes of Nick's things you found at Monty's store?"

"In my car," said Monica. "Let's go get them."

"I don't expect any more crime on the set," Rick reassured her as they walked out of the theater to the parking lot. He stood beside the car trunk as she opened it and removed the two shoe boxes. "What's in them?" he asked with a grin on his face.

"Well, the lid sort of slipped off the top box, and I saw photos and a few letters," she confessed.

"Lids often slip off, I've noticed," he said cheerily.

"Leslie said the same thing."

"I'll call you later," called out Rick. He gave her a jaunty wave as he left her and walked to his car.

Monica hummed to herself as she returned to the theater. Perhaps tomorrow he'd tell her exactly what was in the shoe boxes, but tonight she'd concentrate on being in the opera.

12

On Thursday after school, Monica decided to give Mitsey a special treat. She felt rather guilty because she had been gone so much with the rehearsals at night and as a result neglected to spend special time with her dog.

Although Mitsey was a forgiving creature, Monica wanted to show her a special time tonight by taking her to dinner at the Flying Star restaurant which had an outdoor patio where pets were welcome. When Mitsey heard the words Flying Star, she danced in circles and huffed in anticipation of a dinner out.

Feeling comfortable in jeans and a sweat shirt, Monica grabbed Mitsey's leash and left her apartment with her dog. In a spurt of high spirits and energy, Monica dashed for the car. Catching the excitement, Mitsey galloped behind her.

Monica opened the back door, and Mitsey leaped inside. As soon as she started the engine, Monica lowered the window in the back a couple inches so Mitsey could stick her nose out.

During the trip, Monica noticed a cool draft blasting her neck from the backseat. Mitsey had plunked her black paw on the button to lower the window. The dog's head and half of its body leaned precariously out of an entirely open window. Mitsey had learned a new trick. Quickly Monica raised the window so just a black head could jut out.

At the Flying Star, Monica leashed Mitsey and entered the patio where several other dog owners were sitting with their pets. Everyone appeared to be well-behaved. After hooking the leash to a pole, Monica went into the restaurant to order dinner. Mitsey sat down and checked out the other dogs.

When Monica returned, she carried a bowl of water and a Dr. Pepper. They both took a sip and relaxed until Mitsey spotted Rick reading a newspaper and eating ice cream at a table nearby. After seeing her treat giver, Mitsey wagged her tail and whined.

Hearing a familiar sound, Rick looked up and saw Mitsey and Monica. He walked over, scratched Mitsey's ears, and said, "What a nice surprise. My two favorite girls."

"Hello Rick, please sit down. Mitsey and I are going to have a little dinner." Monica hoped she didn't sound too, too happy. She remembered the advice of all the dating columnists who discouraged excessive female eagerness.

Rick brought his unfinished ice cream dish over to her table and sat down. In a few minutes the waiter arrived with a hamburger and a chef's salad. Monica removed the bun, pickle, and onion before placing the hamburger on the floor for Mitsey.

"That dog eats pretty well," commented Rick.

"I wanted to give her a special treat. She's been neglected a lot since I've been at rehearsals. I guess I'm a little crazy to buy a hamburger for her," confessed Monica. She knew some people believed dogs should only eat prepared dog food. She hoped Rick wasn't one of them.

"Would she like a little bit of ice cream for dessert?" asked Rick.

"Oh, yes, she'd love it," gushed Monica who felt relieved to find out Rick was liberal in the feeding of dogs. He lowered his dish that held a couple spoonfuls of strawberry ice cream. A red tongue immediately started licking the bowl.

"Any news on the case?" asked Monica who forked a piece of tomato into her mouth.

"We're collecting information, nothing significant," he said evasively.

"I know you can't talk about the case to civilians, but I thought I'd ask just in case you could mention just a tiny bit of information, like the contents of those shoe boxes." Monica hoped he might open up and reveal a pertinent clue.

"Just photographs and a couple letters," replied Rick. " I'd like your opinion. Did Nick seem the type who would blackmail somebody?"

"Yes, I got the feeling while he sawed or painted in the back part of the stage, he was constantly listening. I think he heard or saw something about Rob's murder." Monica took another bite of lettuce with a hunk of hard-boiled egg.

"Why do you think he told you he had some information that could be significant if he were the blackmailer himself? He wouldn't want us to catch the killer because it would end his income stream." Rick leaned back in his chair while he questioned Monica.

"I've wondered about that myself. Either he wasn't the blackmailer, or he wanted to throw me off by pointing a finger at an innocent person." Monica had read about clever killers who gave detectives misinformation. "What do you think?"

"I believe Nick was the blackmailer who attempted to make a clever move by tossing out a red herring. I doubt Rob's murderer overheard the conversation in which Nick indicated to you he was going to reveal something important."

"You may be right. I just got carried away by all the fiction I've read. It's really a cliche to have the character say he knows who the killer is, and then he's shot before he can utter the name." Monica added, "Probably the murderer got tired of paying out more money." She twirled her fork around a long piece of lettuce before popping it in her mouth.

"Usually blackmailers can't stop. They think they can go on forever. Often they even increase the amount of each payment without realizing their victims might retaliate violently," Rick said while he loosened his tie.

Monica nodded as she glanced up at him. "You're right, I'm sure." Their eyes met and she felt a little glow warm her face.

After a couple seconds, he said, "But enough of somber news. I'm looking forward to enjoying the music tomorrow night. As I've said before, *Carmen* is one of my favorite operas."

Rick let one arm fall to his side to pick up the empty dish. His fingers got a soft slurp as a thank you from a black and white furry face.

Monica's cell phone chirped. When she answered it, Hugh's voice had an agitated edge. He spoke rapidly, "Monica, I hate to call you at this time, but I have an emergency."

"What is it?"

"I'm supposed to be at the theater for a meeting with Cap and Llorona. He wants her to go through some mumbo jumbo tonight. I can't be there because I just got a call from Belinda who's hysterical and says she has completely lost her voice. Will you go down there and watch whatever crazy claptrap she does?" Hugh's voice sounded strained to Monica's ears.

"Sure, I'll go over there. Don't worry about it, Hugh. I'm sure you can calm Belinda down. She probably just wants attention," answered Monica.

When Monica told Rick about the situation, he chuckled. "I'd like to see that mumbo jumbo myself."

"Come along," she urged.

"I might later, but I have an interview coming up. See you later." He waved as he drifted out of the patio on his way to the parking lot.

About 30 minutes later, Monica parked her car in front of the stage door. "I won't be too long. Just take a little nap," she said to Mitsey whose brown eyes pleaded she wanted to go, too. Monica shook her head and slammed the car door.

When Monica arrived at the stage door, she found it partially open. She guessed Cap wanted to get a breeze going to cool off the place since it was a warm day.

On the stage, Cap held a camera and appeared to be telling Llorona how he planned on filming her ritual. He gestured with his hands indicating where he wanted her to stand.

Llorona wore a long, red velvet cape with a gold embroidered hood which covered most of her gray hair. A red silk gown with four or five strands of gold chains completed her glitzy ensemble. She carried a staff with a large jewel on the top that twinkled in the light like a red beacon.

Monica decided she either looked like a shepherdess who won the lottery or the madam of a Las Vegas brothel.

"Darling," Llorona purred when she saw Monica, "you've come to see me work. I've agreed to come back because this man wants to purify this theater. I would never agree to be on TV for vanity, but only to help him and, of course, the world at large. This place is full of unease. I feel the vibrations, the undulating waves of restlessness coming from the spirits."

"Good, good," said Cap.

Llorona waved her jeweled staff high in the air. "Every time I breathe, I inhale anxiety." Cap moved around in order to film her from different angles.

Llorona stepped slowly in a circle while huffing loudly. She held her staff like the baton of a majorette who's leading the band. Suddenly she stopped. "I feel a presence," she hissed in a hushed voice.

A black dog with a white spot over each eye leaped across the stage and jumped on Monica. Pleased with herself for finding her human mother, Mitsey wagged her tail and licked Monica's hand.

"Where did this nasty creature come from?" shrieked Llorona. "My concentration, my vibrations are gone."

"Nasty creature? Mitsey is a sweet, loveable dog," huffed Monica.

"What is she doing here? Why did you let her in?"

"I didn't let her in. She probably used her paw to get the car window open when I wasn't looking," guessed Monica. After a fleeting greeting, Mitsey ran down the stage stairs and into the dark audience area.

"Get her out!" shouted Llorona.

Monica fumed. She wanted to refuse, but she thought better of it. "I'll go get her leash," she said while walking toward the stage door.

Cap remained quiet during all of the dither. He looked at Llorona's pursed lips and angry eyes and said politely, "Would you like to sit for a minute? I'll get a chair."

"No, I don't want to sit," she answered with her arms crossed over her chest.

Monica returned with her leash and called out, "Here, Mitsey." Since only the stage lights were on, Monica couldn't see the dog so she just shouted into darkness.

Cap went over to the light board and fussed about as he tried to light up the audience area. Monica heard snuffles and galloping feet coming from the dark, but the sounds didn't appear to be coming toward her. She heard scrabbling between the rows of seats, down the aisles, into the lobby and in a few minutes, the sounds of a running dog returning toward the stage.

Short little yelps and pounding paws suddenly came from backstage. Monica wondered if Mitsey was chasing a critter of some sort. She remained on the stage while waiting for Cap to light up the place.

New human sounds came from the stage door. Monica heard whispering.

"Do you think we should go in?"

"Why not? Let's just check it out." Two college students tiptoed to the edge of the lighted stage. They dragged their signs that said, "Don't Evict the Ghost."

Monica recognized Leroy, one of the protestors. "Hi, Leroy," she called out in a friendly voice.

"Hi," he answered. But after first looking at Monica, his eyes focused on the creature in red. "We just thought we'd come in for a minute so we could see The Spot."

"Young man, you should be studying for your finals," scolded Llorona.

"We don't have finals until December," answered Leroy. After staring at her for another minute, he asked, "Are you in the show?"

"No, of course not. I'm a seer. I'm here to talk to the ghost."

"Wow! This is our lucky day," exclaimed Leroy.

The other student, evidently less impressed with the mighty red seer than her companion, was concentrating on the floor boards. "Look at the dark spots over there. Is that where it happened?"

"Yes," answered Monica.

"Wow," the two students said in unison. Everyone looked at The Spot in silence.

"Hugh said the floor will be painted before the show tomorrow night, and no one will see anything," explained Monica.

"I'm glad we came now so we could see it," said Leroy. "I'm also glad I got to meet you, ma'am. I've never met a real seer before."

Llorona smiled benevolently, shook off her hood, and stretched out her hand. "My name is Llorona the Good."

Leroy shook her hand, "Leroy Marx. Pleased to meet you. I can't believe I'm right here talking to a seer. I've read about Tiresias and a few others, but, wow, you're a real one!"

Llorona preened. "Dear boy, come over here, and let's sit down and chat a bit."

While all this new activity took place, Monica forgot about rounding up her errant dog. No one else mentioned the dog either.

Cap had finally figured out the proper light switches, and the entire theater was ablaze in light. He picked up his camera and walked over to Llorona who was telling Leroy about all her contacts with the spirits from the Other World.

Cap barged in on their conversation, "Pardon me, but do you think the phantom is still here?"

"I'll summon him. Perhaps he is angry, perhaps not," Llorona declared. She stood by The Spot, shut her eyes, and inhaled. As before, she circled the area while breathing loudly and mumbling some words. "'Thrice the brindled cat hath mewed,/ Thrice, and once the hedge-pig whine./ Harpier cries, 'Tis time, 'tis time.'" After three laps, she lifted the bejeweled staff high with her right arm.

Monica knew she used the lines from the witches' speech in Act IV of Shakespeare's *Macbeth*. At least she's quoting from the best thought Monica and not just babbling Latin.

As everyone silently watched and listened, Monica wondered how Llorona would manage tonight's hocus-pocus charade. She couldn't have set up any tricks beforehand since Cap had picked her up and driven her to the theater.

Llorona took out just one black candle this time. After she lit the candle and a stick of incense, a heavy scent filled the air. Monica tried to hold back a sneeze, but couldn't. Llorona shot her a baleful look but quickly went back to staring at the candle.

After a dramatic flick of her staff at The Spot, Llorona said, "'Then the charm is firm and good.'" Llorona raised her arms and tilted her head to the ceiling. In a loud voice she commanded, "Speak!"

The you-could-hear-a-pin-drop silence extended for several seconds until a loud response was heard. "Woof, woof."

A dog from backstage and not the phantom from the Other World had answered. Monica bit her lip to keep from laughing since she knew her dog's bark wouldn't be considered funny. Carefully she started to tiptoe away from the little group watching big red so she could catch Mitsey.

As she looked towards the woofing direction, she heard an eerie voice moan, "Vengeance." Each syllable was elongated and raspy. Monica tried to pinpoint where the voice came from, but it seemed to come from everywhere. It wailed once more the same word followed by a creepy squeal.

Llorona stood like a statue. The members of the tiny group didn't move a muscle except Leroy who made the sign of the cross.

The ghoulish moment was broken when Mitsey flew across the stage, gave Monica a slurp on her hand, leaped down the stage stairs, and once again charged up the aisle in the audience seating area. Mitsey was having fun.

Cap spoke first, "That was great! I got everything. Tell me who was it?"

"The phantom. I'm worn out. Summoning the spirits is so hard on my body. You don't know what I go through when I have these seances. I must sit down." Llorona slumped down in a folding chair while Cap hovered over her.

"Next time could you ask if the phantom likes it here? Tell him I'm trying to keep him from being evicted," Leroy piped up.

"Not now, Leroy," cautioned Monica.

"What did the phantom mean about vengeance. Vengeance has been done or will be done?" Cap mused aloud. "I'll start my program with that question. The audience will love it. Of course, I'll be filming the opera tomorrow night just in case something happens." Cap capered around while he checked his equipment to make sure he got a good sound byte of the phantom's voice.

Monica kept wondering how in the hell she did it. Not for a moment did she think that the phantom or the spook or the whatever spoke. She kept her thoughts to herself since she had told Hugh she would keep her mouth shut for the sake of the opera.

Her immediate problem, getting the dog, needed attention. "Here, Mitsey, here Mitsey," she shouted as she walked down the stage steps into the audience seating area.

"Mitsey, Mitsey," she kept repeating, but no dog appeared.

After several minutes, she heard Rick's voice. "Mitsey's over here."

"When did you come in?" asked Monica as she made her way back to the stage again.

"I just walked in and heard you call the dog. She's right here, sitting down, and waiting for you," he replied. When Monica climbed up the stairs again, there sat Mitsey panting in big huffs with a smile on her face. As she got closer, she noticed a trailing red ribbon with dried rose petals entangled on Mitsey's collar.

Rick examined the ribbon. "I wonder where she got this?"

"She's been all over the place," answered Monica as she removed the ribbon and petals from the dog's collar.

"Let's try to find where she got this ribbon. It might have something to do with the case," said Rick.

"Something else happened that might be important. The spook spoke," declared Monica, "and that's not easy to say."

Rick repeated the words, "The spook spoke." He chuckled. "That's quite a tongue twister, but I want to hear all the details."

Monica related the event and ended her account with the question that had been bothering her. "How did she do it?"

"We'll have to check everything out." Rick appeared to be more interested in the dried rose petals that had fallen on the floor than Llorona's chicanery. As he fingered the ribbon, Monica noticed it had once been part of a bow and had a couple thorny stems still caught in the fabric.

"Let's take a look to see if we can find more rose petals," suggested Rick as he gave the dog a pat. He quickly surveyed the floor while Monica drifted to the back areas where the props were stacked. There she saw a few specks of dried petals.

"I see some," she shouted. "This is just like Hansel and Gretel following the bread crumbs." She became excited as she saw a few more in the back. Rick walked over to her and spotted a few himself. During all this time, Mitsey danced around them and snuffled some dust bunnies her movements had dislodged.

At the very end of the space, they found shelving with boxes with various labels: candle holders, table clothes, Christmas decorations, nails, tape, etc.

Between these boxes other things had been stuck wherever they fit. A table lamp had been squeezed into one space, a small vase into another.

On the bottom shelf, Monica noticed a box had fallen over. When she stooped and peered in it, she saw a little nest made out of dried rose petals. "Look, Rick, a mouse must have been here. I bet Mitsey heard a noise and knocked over the box."

The box overflowed with more red ribbon and dried petals. Monic fished around in the scraps and discovered a photo of a young man sitting on a wall and smiling at the camera. In the corner was written, "To my love, Rob"

"It's a picture of the dead Rob," said Monica.

Rick bent down and examined the box. "This could have been a letter exchange place for Rob and his lover. We never found out who she was. Various people said Rob had a mysterious sweetheart because at times he mentioned 'my darling lark.' We thought perhaps she was a singer because of the bird reference, but, of course, lovers have all sorts of secret names for each other. I'll take all of this with me and hope we can find fingerprints, but I doubt it."

Monica had to give Mitsey credit for the find. "Good dog, you found a clue," she said to her. Mitsey wagged her tail and sniffed the area again. When Rick and Monica walked back to center stage, Llorona was still sitting on the folding chair.

She tilted her head while her hand touched her forehead. "Oh, my head, it aches from all the concentration. If you are a psychic like I am, then you feel the spirit's unhappiness, the suffering. Sometimes I wish I didn't have The Gift. But I must bear the pain. It is my lot in life." Llorona spoke as if she held the burden of the world on her shoulders.

While the oracle complained about the difficulties of possessing transcendental powers, Cap filmed her.

Monica admired the way Llorona positioned herself in such a glamorous way on such a hard, ordinary folding chair. While she leaned back, she kept her hand gracefully arched over her eye. She had good instincts for publicity.

Mitsey looked at the lady in red, raised her ears, tipped her head, and howled.

"There's that dreadful dog again. Take him away," hissed Llorona who snapped to attention and glowered at the baying dog.

"Sorry," said Monica through clenched teeth, while she tugged at Mitsey's leash. Monica thought Mitsey did what any dog would do after seeing such a weird woman.

Rick distracted Mitsey by whistling a come-let's-go shrill toot. Mitsey galloped over to him followed by Monica who almost tripped when the dog surged forward. The three exited together leaving the prophetess and her new disciples in the theater.

13

As soon as they were outside, Monica turned to Rick. "How did she do it? The big phony rigged up that overly dramatic voice so she could be on Cap's TV program. Do you think she fooled Cap, or maybe he doesn't care as long as he gets a good audience rating?"

"She must have put in a recording device somewhere in the stage area. I think Cap wasn't fooled, but he has to put on a show. He's spent a lot of money by coming out here with his team so he's going to pretend Albuquerque has a phantom of the opera."

Monica said, "Haunted houses, theaters or whatever interests people. I don't care for this ghoulish type of entertainment, but teenagers especially like programs about vampires, werewolves, ghosts, zombies, and scary creatures." Monica knew the reading habits of teenagers very well. They complained all the time that *Jane Eyre* wasn't as good as a zombie book.

Rick walked Monica to her car and opened the back door first so Mitsey could jump in before he opened the front door for Monica. As she cracked the back window for the dog, she smiled at Rick. "Finding the murderer is more important than figuring out Llorona's tricks, but both are puzzles I'd like to solve. See you later."

Rick leaned in as if he were going to kiss her, but backed away when he saw a few people on the street. "I'll call you. Bye."

When Monica returned home, her phone was ringing. She picked up the receiver, and Hugh's voice said, "I have to find out what happened at the theater tonight. If there was a crisis, don't tell me. Yes, tell me, but break it to me gently. I can't stand any more tension. Thank God, Belinda's over her little snit."

"Everything is fine, Hugh. Don't worry. Cap crowed about Llorona's show. I was impressed when she had the ghost speak 'Vengeance' in an eerie, raspy voice. I don't know how she did it, but Cap recorded it." Monica spoke in low, measured tones since Hugh sounded like a worrywart again.

"Good. I'm going to take a couple aspirins and go to bed. Thanks, Monica." Hugh sounded relieved as he hung up.

Monica had hardly set the receiver down when the phone rang again. She sighed and lifted the receiver.

"My name is Jack Jones, the Fridge Magnet King. I've been manufacturing fridge magnets for years. I work right here in Albuquerque, and I want to make a nice souvenir for the opera using this phantom thing. I was talking to Cap tonight, and he gave me Hugh's name and yours. Hugh is not answering his phone, and I need to speak to someone in authority."

"I'm not an authority," said Monica.

"You can give me an opinion, at least. I want this fridge magnet to be special. People love the idea that Albuquerque has its own phantom of the opera. I don't want to use a man with a white patch over one side of his face. I want an original phantom. What do you think about a twirling brown spirit?"

"Too much like a dust devil," said Monica as she nixed the idea.

"No good. Okay, how about a traditional white sheeted figure with lonely eyes?"

"Too much like Halloween. Do you want a menacing spirit or a cute one?" Monica started to get interested in finding the right tone for the Albuquerque spook.

"Pleasing, but not cute. Scary in a non-threatening way."

"That's a very delicate balance you're trying to find. How about a purple figure with swirling mist? The figure could have a hood of some sort that hides his face. Not having a visible face would make the phantom more ambiguous, neither attractive nor horrible."

"I like it. I like it."

"On second thought, perhaps it isn't a good idea. The hood with a dark space for the face could resemble a common drawing of death." Monica paused. "I'm sorry. I really can't come up with a good logo. Also, I'm tired." She yawned as she cradled the receiver between her ear and shoulder.

"Actually, you gave me a couple ideas. If I work at it tonight, I can paint a couple hundred fridge magnets. I'd like to sell them on opening night. I'm donating 10% of my sales to the opera company for allowing me to sell in the lobby."

"I'll make a point of checking out what design you came up with," replied Monica who sat down and kicked off her shoes. "See you tomorrow before the show."

After she turned off the phone, her cats walked over the back of her sofa, plopped in her lap, and purred. Monica used a hand to pet each cat and even a foot to stroke Mitsey who was lying at her feet. She felt it was important to show love to all her pets so they wouldn't become delinquents.

On opening night, Monica went to the lobby before getting ready for the show in order to satisfy her curiosity about how the Fridge Magnet King portrayed the ghost.

The magnets lay on a black velvet cloth on a long table in the center of the lobby. He had painted the words "Albuquerque's Phantom of the Opera"on a black background with the figure dressed in deep purple with a white cowboy hat and a white eye mask. Monica immediately thought of the Lone Ranger or a Western Batman.

"What do you think? Classy, solid, eye-catching. I'm selling them at $10 a pop." Jack whipped out a handkerchief and wiped off some imaginary dust from one and adjusted the placement of another.

Another magnet style had "Carmen" painted at the top and showed a beautiful gypsy girl with a coquettish tip of the head. In the background behind a curtain, a purple figure with a cowboy hat lurked. The third style just had a picture of Carmen without a shadowy phantom.

"They're great, Jack."

"Which do you think will be the most popular?"

"I'm guessing right now everyone is intrigued with the phantom, and you'll sell the one where he's displayed alone." The more Monica looked at the figure, the more she thought he came across as a vigilante, a good guy.

"That's what I thought. I made 50 more of that one," boasted Jack who sat down behind his table and checked his money drawer.

"Has Belinda seen the magnets?" asked Monica. She hoped Belinda wouldn't see them because she knew what her reaction would be. All magnets, all publicity, all thoughts, all eyes should be on the star. The phantom wasn't a criminal. He was worse. He was a scene stealer.

The Magnet King said, "No one has seen them, except you, of course. I worked on those puppies for hours. I used stencils, but still I used my artistic talent when I designed them."

Monica glanced out the window of the lobby and saw Leroy with his protest sign. She waved at him, and he came over to the door. "Come on in and see the magnets Jack made last night," she said.

Leroy opened the door, saw the magnets, and grinned his approval. "Those are great. I like the phantom. He looks like a hero, like the Lone Ranger."

Jack said, "Thank you, my boy. I hope others will like them and buy them."

"Could you make some tee shirts with the phantom? My friends and I plan to picket every performance of the show. If we could wear tee shirts with his picture, I'm sure it'd be more effective." Leroy picked up the magnet and studied it.

"I'm the Fridge Magnet King, but I also expand on good ideas. Do you really think tee shirts would go over?"

"Yes, yes. I'm getting more of my buddies to help the protest, and they'll want to wear them." Leroy spoke with confidence.

"Do you really think the ghost is being evicted?" asked Monica.

Leroy narrowed his eyes and inhaled deeply. "Yes, yesterday I talked with the red seer woman. As

I was leaving, I overheard a conversation. She's going to chuck out the phantom because Cap gave her some money to do it. Can you believe she's forcing him out just for filthy money?"

"Are you sure? When I left with Mitsey and Rick, she hadn't said anything about getting rid of the phantom. She just wanted to communicate with him." Monica hadn't heard about this new twist.

"After you left, Cap asked if she could do an exorcism. She said it was very difficult, very hard on her, and very expensive. He said he'd pay her what she wanted. She agreed just like that. She has no ethics and doesn't even consider the phantom's feelings." While Leroy explained the dirty deal that was made, he furrowed his brow and tightened his lips in displeasure.

Monica nodded her head. "Money is a strong motivator, Leroy."

Leroy said in a snippy voice, "I suppose it is for *some* people." Monica noted the way he emphasized the word *some* implied he was above such things. The clothes he wore certainly indicated a lack of interest in finery. He wore jeans with holes, dirty tennis shoes, and a faded tee shirt with a picture of a dragon.

Monica tried to divert his attention by holding up the Carmen magnet. Leroy glanced at it and looked down at the velvet cloth with all the magnets laid out in neat rows.

The Fridge Magnet King looked at his stock as he asked Leroy, "Which design do you want for the tee shirts?"

Leroy showed no hesitation. "The one with him alone. He looks good."

"I'll get that design made tonight, and I'll have the tee shirts for you by 4:00 tomorrow. You'll have plenty of time to put them on before you start your picketing. Meet me here in front of the theater."

Monica was impressed Jack could switch to another medium and produce a large number of items so quickly. She had a thought that might jeopardize this new business. "What if Llorona says the exorcism worked? Albuquerque won't have its own phantom."

Jack turned to Leroy. "Listen, son, can you do something to make this exorcism fizzle?"

Leroy blinked a couple times and looked at Monica. "How could we stop it?"

Monica didn't know how to respond to this appeal. She decided she had to be honest and not perpetuate this hooey. "You can't stop her from coming. She could say anything or do anything she wants and proclaim the spook is gone because she's a quack."

"But what about last night? I heard the ghost. Didn't you hear him?" Leroy looked at her in confusion.

"It was a trick," said Monica. "I don't know how she did it, but it has to be a trick."

"Let's go with the flow," advised Jack. "We'll worry about the lady's abilities later. People like the idea of the phantom. Go on, kid, go picket. Don't worry."

Monica decided no one wanted to hear a word about any type of hoax. Having a phantom of the opera in Albuquerque was profitable and kind of fun.

Monica peered at her watch and said, "Sorry, I've got to go and get my makeup on. See you later." She darted out the lobby door and headed for the stage entrance. As she walked, she greeted other members of the cast.

Once inside, Monica heard the sounds of pre-show jitters and snippets of music. A couple violins went through the G scale. The tympanist had his ear to his drum as he started tuning it. Meredith hit a high C, and Belinda chattered about bad air in the dressing room.

Monica noticed Llorona wore a long black gown without any jewelry. Perhaps she used different colors for different types of paranormal activity. She, Hugh, and Cap were huddled together in a corner by the table with coffee and tea.

Monica pretended she needed a drink so she could amble over and sort of scoot a few inches at a time to overhear the conversation.

"What's wrong with an exorcism? It will make everyone feel more comfortable before the opera starts," argued Cap. He carried his camera over his shoulder and looked eager to start filming. A member of his team stood beside him and carried a couple lights.

"It will spook, sorry to use that word, my singers. Belinda is very sensitive. I don't want her thinking about any phantom before she goes on stage," retorted Hugh.

"I don't know if I can work with all this hubbub. An exorcism is a serious ritual which should be done in silence," said Llorona

"Silence is impossible before a show," Hugh said.

Cap began arguing, "Go ahead, my dear, give it a try. My TV audience wants to see you. I can start my show by saying that before the first performance of *Carmen,* an exorcism was held to protect the cast. If the ghost refuses to leave, I'll say Llorona will use even stronger means for the next exorcism." Cap ended his latest argument by adding, "I'll throw in a couple hundred bucks extra."

Llorona hesitated, sighed, and said, "Well, I could try."

Hugh shrugged his shoulders and shook his head. "I want everyone to know I'm against it. I don't want my singers distracted before a performance."

Llorona paid no attention to Hugh. She opened her big black tote and took out a black candle which she lit. After walking to The Spot, she set the candle down on the floor and raised both her hands into the air and chanted in Latin. People quieted down to see what in the world the oracle woman was going to do this time.

A few whispered, "It's an exorcism. She's trying to get rid of the phantom."

Monica, glad about Belinda's absence, sat down in a folding chair and waited for the chicanery.

Monica wanted to ask Llorona about her chants. Sometimes they were in Latin, and other times she used snippets from *Macbeth* in English. Were there recipes with a stated language, placement of arms, number of candles, flavor of incense, and color of costume? Did she have a special book of spells?

Currently she was making the "come here" wave with her hand while looking at the ceiling light. Monica thought that gesture was rather trite. Surely, she could come up with a better paranormal looking way of inviting a ghost to come forward.

"Woo, woo," a strange voice wailed. Monica turned her head from side to side in an effort to locate where it came from. A figure in a white sheet with open eye slits stood in the wings and keened again, "Woo, woo." Slowly it began to run across the stage. Monica could see black pants and black dress shoes under the bottom of the sheet.

"Woo, woo, I'm going to get you," moaned the white, new arrival.

It waved its arms so high that the sheet billowed and undulated. When it got to the end of the stage, it descended down the side steps. It kept wooing while thrashing around in the aisles between the seats in the audience area.

Everyone silently watched the antics of the ghostly presence until a spurt of laughter erupted from the orchestra pit. The drummer had his hand over his mouth while he snorted in merriment. The wooing figure running toward the lobby started to guffaw. The sheet fell off and revealed the clarinet player.

It cracked everyone up. In their hilarity, people slapped the bogus ghost on the back and gave him a couple high fives. The sax player picked up the fallen sheet and did a bit of woo wooing himself.

While Monica was laughing, she noticed Llorona crossing her arms over her chest and pursing her lips into a grimace. The oracle was not amused. After several minutes, the cast members' initial burst of wild merriment descended into chuckles and giggles.

The psychic shouted to Hugh, "How can I do a decent exorcism under these circumstances? Fire that young man immediately!"

Hugh, still laughing, ignored Llorona. He spoke to the cast, "Let's get ready for the show and forget about all this spook business."

Llorona remained angry. "Why wasn't that young man fired?"

Hugh diplomatically said, "I'm sorry he interrupted you, but everyone has first night jitters. I'm sure he meant no harm, just a bit of youthful hijinks."

"Hijinks? Hijinks? He showed disrespect to me and my Gift. I don't like this place. I don't know why any spirit would want to stay here. I certainly don't. I'm leaving." She picked up her candle, put it in her tote, and huffed off.

Cap ran after her, but she paid no attention to him. After Llorona had huffed out, Cap went into the pit and scolded the clarinet player. He kept saying, "I have a serious show. I don't want laughs. People want to see real live ghosts."

Monica pondered what he meant by wanting *real live ghosts*. She thought it was an excellent example of an oxymoron like jumbo shrimp, cruel kindness, and bitter sweet. The news had also made a new oxymoron which the entire nation enjoyed, legitimate rape.

Needing to put on her toga and her theatrical makeup, Monica walked towards the dressing room. Briefly she considered consoling Cap, but decided he should lighten up. In under an hour the curtain would rise so she switched her thoughts to the opera. Would anything happen on opening night?

14

Monica parted a tiny bit of the stage curtain and peeked at the audience. She knew it was considered bad luck, but she couldn't resist. Many of the patrons were talking in the aisles and not sitting down promptly when they entered.

After a wait of ten minutes, Hugh gave the signal. The conductor took his position, lifted his baton, and started the overture. The members of the audience hushed when they heard the beautiful, familiar music. The few still standing quickly sat down.

The curtain rose and revealed the Jesus Christ Sandal Factory and the guard house of the Roman centurions. Everyone clapped after viewing the set design.

In the first scene, Meredith wore a fitted pink toga costume with a low neckline and a short skirt. Instead of the big hunk of cloth draped over a shoulder, Meredith's costume had just a bit of cloth draped to the waist. The drape didn't cross over her body, but sort of hung loosely. Both of her shapely legs were quite visible when she moved.

Standing in the wings while waiting for the entrance of the chorus, Monica looked down at her unattractive, baggy costume. She and the other women wore traditional togas with lots of white cloth draped over one shoulder.

After Meredith, as Flavia, left the stage, the centurions arrived for the changing of the guards. Milt, as Joseimus, wore a deep purple tunic with a cord belt of silver. Against the white tunics of the rest of the soldiers, his purple one put him in the limelight. Milt stood straight and tall while he and the officer exchanged information about Flavia.

As they sang, Monica noticed Milt had a tendency to step forward a couple inches in front of the officer.

After hearing their cue, Monica and the chorus girls sauntered on stage. They pretended to light their candy cigarettes and take long puffs. They sang about smoke which gives pleasure but is ephemeral, like words of love. Monica wondered if this song reflected the motivation for the murder of Rob Grainger. Could he have spurned his lover just as Carmen did?

Although the blond Meredith looked beautiful, Monica noticed she lost the attention of the audience when Belinda, as Carmen, haughtily strutted on stage. She flounced her scarlet skirt and seductively pulled one sleeve off her shoulder, lowering the bodice and revealing even more skin than she had during rehearsal.

When Carmen threw the rose at Joseimus as she left, he didn't jig or put it in his mouth. He clasped it to his chest while he sang.

Monica stole a quick glance off to the right wing to see if Hugh was chewing his fingernails. Earlier Hugh had told her he worried about how Milt would perform in this scene. Milt was so unpredictable he might do his celebration of life dance steps even after he agreed not to.

After the bad girl in brilliant scarlet left, the good girl in pale pink came on stage. Monica thought Hugh did a good job of contrasting the colors of the dresses of the two main characters. Husband and wife sang together when Flavia told Joseimus about his mother's prayers and love for him. This touching scene rated a round of applause.

Monica almost started to relax because everything was going so well. She had felt tension before, but the singers and orchestra members were performing the opera like professionals who aren't fazed by murder or spooks.

The only one with a grim face was Cap. Monica thought he probably hoped the phantom would appear, speak, or throw something. His program needed more substantial material or, as she chuckled to herself, less substantial material.

She heard the cue for the cigarette girls to go on stage after the fight in the factory. Carmen, who supposedly had attacked and injured a girl, appeared with several locks of hair awry and more bosom and leg showing. Monica wasn't surprised. Belinda would never appear in real disarray, especially on stage.

When Joseimus was ordered to take her to prison, Carmen flirtatiously suggested they dance and drink wine at the tavern, Lillimus Pastimus, if he would let her go. The audience clapped again after Carmen sang the famous "Seguidilla."

Monica could feel the seductive pull Carmen was having on Joseimus, or was it the seductive pull Belinda was having on Milt Grainger? Sometimes actors and actresses melded with their roles thought Monica.

After the tragic murder of Carmen and the sorrowful lament of Joseimus, the final curtain came down. Monica looked over at Hugh smiling in the wings.

Hugh was not only smiling at the end of the opera, he was beaming. The audience gave a standing ovation to the cast, the stars, and the orchestra.

Belinda and Meredith both received large bouquets of flowers which they cradled in their arms like babies. Milt and Burt looked pleased with the loud bursts of applause when they made their curtain calls.

After all these bows, Hugh turned on the hall lights. The audience members gathered up their belongings, while the singers started hugging each other. Monica hugged her fellow chorus girls and randomly other people as well. She felt a flush of the joy of being part of a successful, exciting production.

The hugging kept going. Monica realized she had hugged some people twice, but no matter. Love saturated the air. When Milt hugged her the third time, he asked, "Did they clap louder for me or for Carmen?"

"Much louder for you. Your applause was deafening," answered Monica.

Milt squeezed her waist and leaned his head in for a kiss. Monica mimicked a little cough, and Milt immediately backed off and hurried away.

Opera goers climbed the stage stairs and mingled with the singers which lead to more hugs and congratulations. While all this jubilation bubbled over like champagne, organ music from *The Phantom of the Opera* blared out. When people heard it, they clapped. Monica heard various positive comments.

"Perfect. How clever to play this music for the party."

"It's so exciting. The phantom music adds to the atmosphere."

"Do you think our phantom will make an appearance?"

Monica figured this good-hearted joke had the earmark of the clarinet player and the drummer who probably had hooked up a music disc to the loud speaker.

The caterer's men, dressed in black pants and white shirts, brought in a case of champagne. They set it on the table and started popping corks. People filled the Green Room and spilled over onto the stage itself with all the scenery still in place.

Shrimp, cold meats, and chicken wing platters came in next followed by crackers and cheese. New tables sprung up like mushrooms and became loaded with more food. One of the waiters devoted all his time to opening bottles of champagne. The pop and fizz noises added to the festive atmosphere.

Monica felt the familiar arms of Rick who had just arrived. He not only got a good hug but a long kiss as well. After his greeting, he praised the performance. "Great show! I've seen this opera five or six times, and I never tire of it. The singers, the production, everything was superb."

Rick snagged a couple flutes of champagne as a bustling waiter passed by. Monica took the offered glass and lifted it so they could have the traditional clinking of glasses before they took a sip. Monica let the bubbly wine slip down her throat. A few seconds later she had to put her fingers to her lips to cover a tiny burp.

Another waiter with a full bottle walked by and topped off their glasses. Champagne flowed at a rapid rate. A second case was opened, and the busy waiters kept filling glasses.

Money Man Monty stepped on the stage, walked over to Monica and Rick, and greeted them with his hearty handshake and boisterous greeting, "Hi folks, good to see you again."

Barbara J. Langner

"Monty, what are you doing here?" asked Monica who certainly hadn't expected to see him at an opera. She blushed as she realized she had been rather rude.

Monty didn't appear to be offended in the least. He said, "I love opera. I go to every opera I can. I always have a season ticket to the Santa Fe summer series, and last year I even went to New York for a week of the Met performances. Verdi is probably my favorite composer, but I love Wagner's Ring Cycle, although it can be a bit heavy."

Monty was wearing a navy suit, white shirt with a tie. To Monica, he looked like a regular member of the audience. She realized, of course, he should have enough sense not to wear a green suit with $20 bills sticking out of the pockets.

Rick said, "I've never heard all of the Ring operas, but I do like *Das Rhinegold.*"

"Yes, it's beautiful. Too bad it's not performed much anymore."

"A company in Seattle used to do the entire series during the summer," added Rick while he took another sip of the bubbly. "I wish I had taken time off to hear it."

"I heard it there ten years ago, " said Monty. "It was great. By the way, I'm closing down my book business, and I'm going to follow my dream. A man has to reach for the gold ring and aim for the stars. A man has to have fire in his belly and do what he wants to do."

Monica felt like rolling her eyes at his string of cliches.

Rick politely asked, "What do you want to be?"

"A pimp," he answered and added, "I probably shouldn't tell you, since you're a policeman and all, but it's always been my dream. I'll take the night off

- 152 -

whenever an opera is in town. During Christmas vacation, I'll go to New York and hit the Met again."

"Do the ladies of the night, or should I use the new word, *hos*, get Christmas vacation?" asked the curious Monica.

"Of course, they need time for Christmas shopping. In my business, I'll also provide Thanksgiving and Easter vacations. I'll run my shop more or less on a school calendar. The girls, however, can't expect to have a long two-month summer vacation. They'll get just a week or so." Monty paused and furrowed his brow.

When Monica looked at Rick, he had a bemused expression on his face. He said, "You might start a new trend in the pimp business by giving the girls school vacations."

Monica noticed Rick's eyes were twinkling, and the corners of his mouth started to turn up. After his humorous reaction to Monty's news, his voice became serious. "In some locations prostitution is legal, but not here in Albuquerque."

"I know. I haven't decided where I'll set up shop." Monty grabbed a glass of champagne, tipped it up, and swallowed it all. "I'd like to encourage the girls to join a city bowling league. It would be a healthy exercise, besides being lots of fun. It could be an afternoon activity since, of course, they work at night."

Monty's eyes roved around. "Just a second, I see sliced beef over there on the table. I haven't eaten for awhile. I'm going to make a sandwich."

After Monty had walked away, Rick turned to Monica. "I've never had such a bizarre conversation before. Is this guy for real?"

"He's very strange, but don't you think he has some new refreshing ideas about how he's going to run his bordello. I've read a few novels like *Cannery Row* that include descriptions of life in a brothel and in none of them did the girls bowl in a league."

Monica thought for a moment and said, "Tonight at Albuquerque Alleys, Bed Bath and Beyond plays the Cat House."

Rick chimed in with another version. "How about P. F. Chang plays the House of Ho?"

Both Monica and Rick burst into laughter again. A waiter walked by and filled Monica's glass again. After taking another sip, she added. "I don't think Monty is going to be successful in his new career."

Rick said, "He definitely isn't going to fit in well with his pimp colleagues. I venture to say not one of them will ask him if he prefers Verdi's *Rigoletto* to *Il Trovatore*. I predict his business career will be very short."

"He can always return to selling his books on how to make a million dollars. Earlier he told me he's keeping his money tree along with all those boxes of books he hasn't sold."

A waiter came by with a platter of shrimp with a bowl of sauce in the middle. Monica and Rick each reached out and speared a shrimp with the provided toothpicks.

"By the way," said Rick, "I like the organ music in the background for the party. Nice touch. Who thought of it?"

"I don't know. Everyone seems to be enjoying the phantom thing. Cap and his team keep hoping for manifestations of paranormal activity, and I think the audience would like a little thrill, too. Nothing awful, but just a little something to give a tingle." Monica popped a shrimp in her mouth and licked her lips.

"Piping in organ music is atmospheric, but I doubt anyone is getting a tingle," said Rick who ate another shrimp.

Monica glanced around at the people chattering, eating, and still hugging. Burt Brown had one arm around a chorus boy in a smuggler's costume, and Milt was chatting up Belinda. Monica presumed the two had quit giving each other little digs.

She noticed the Fridge Magnet King piling slices of turkey on a Kaiser roll and talking to Monty. The two men, holding their sandwiches, walked back to Monica and Rick.

"Hi, I'm Jack Jones," said the Fridge Magnet King as he held out his hand to Rick. "You know, this young lady here inspired the design for my Albuquerque phantom. I sold out during the intermission. I'm going to make some tee shirts for those kids who are picketing out in front. Hey, look, they came in for the food." Jack pointed at the buffet table.

Monica saw Leroy Marx and five of his buddies munching sandwiches and potato chips. As she watched, they helped themselves to champagne. "Rick, those college kids are probably underage. Should I intervene or look the other way?"

Rick replied, "I don't see any underage kids drinking alcohol."

"You're right. I don't see any either," Monica said and sighed with relief. She really didn't want to make a scene.

"Naw, those kids are okay. Let them have a taste of the bubbly," Jack said.

Monty agreed. "I spoke to them, and they said protest initiates a change in attitudes. I guess they're taking a sociology class at the University."

Jack took a bite of his sandwich. "They asked me to do a phantom tee shirt for them. I bet I can sell them to the audience, too. I've been talking to Monty here, and I think I've been too restrictive in my business. I concentrated too much on my fridge magnets. I love 'em, but I've got to branch out. Besides tee shirts, I'm going to make some day planners for Monty."

"Actually," Monty pointed out, "not day planners but night planners. Black leather with pink lettering. I might use the same colors for my bowling shirts."

"I never thought the ladies would like embossed leather time planners, but I realize they might appreciate your thoughtfulness," said Monica. She deliberately didn't look at Rick for fear she'd break up.

The Fridge Magnet King came up with another suggestion. "How about a design on your bowling shirts?"

Monty scratched his chin. "I've been thinking about cats. Maybe cats rolling yarn balls down a bowling alley."

Jack said, "I could prepare a couple designs and show them to you tomorrow. Right now, I've got to leave since I have to print the tee shirts for the protesting kids. They want to wear them tomorrow night." He shook hands with everyone and left.

Monty brushed off a few crumbs of his sandwich that had fallen on his shirt. "By the way, Detective Miller, as I cleaned out my storage unit, I noticed some stuff that isn't mine. You got the couple boxes I had in the back of my store that belonged to Nick, but

I have some more of his stuff in my unit at the Honest Abe Storage. Do you want to check it out?"

"Definitely, could I meet you there tomorrow at 9:00?" asked Rick. Monica saw him perk up when he heard this news.

"Sure, I'll be there. Take all his stuff. I don't want it."

"I'm hoping there might be something that will help us find his killer." Rick rubbed his hands together.

Monty looked at Monica. "Do you want to come, too?"

"Yes, I'd love to, if it's okay with the detective," replied Monica. She was happy that tomorrow was Saturday.

"Why not?" said Rick. He smiled at her and winked.

Monty said, "I'm heading home. See you both tomorrow."

After all the champagne was drunk and the sandwiches eaten, the party started to wind down. The caterers gathered up empty platters and put them in boxes. They threw away paper napkins, shrimp tails, and crumbs of bread. The revelers toddled off either to the stage door or the lobby door.

As Monica and Rick finished eating the last of the potato chips, Cap tapped Monica on the shoulder. "If you see Hugh, tell him I'm staying here for the rest of the night. The spook could still appear."

Monica couldn't think of any encouraging thing to say to him. "Okay, I'll tell him."

Meredith approached Monica just as Cap turned away. "Have you seen Milt? I'm ready to go home, and I can't find him."

"No, I haven't seen him. He might have gone to the dressing room to change."

"I'll take a look," she answered as she hurried away.

"With all these people milling around, Milt could be lost easily," said Monica. "Let's leave. The caterers want to go home, and so do I. I'll quickly change clothes and remove my makeup."

As Monica darted into the women's dressing room, out of the corner of her eye she saw movement at the back of the stage where the props were kept. She tiptoed slowly in that direction and saw Milt kissing Belinda in an erotic embrace. Quickly she turned and walked silently back to the dressing room.

She thought those seductive scenes in the opera must have spilled over into real life. While she was rubbing cold cream on her face, she kept musing about Milt's romancing the lovely Belinda. Was it just a passing fancy? Probably. She switched her thoughts to tomorrow and the prospect of finding a clue at the Honest Abe Storage unit.

15

Situated on the edge of town, the Honest Abe Storage Company sprawled over a couple acres. Huge cottonwood trees gave shade to the main building and the rows of rental units during most of the day. As Monica drove into the parking lot, her car tires crunched on the gravel.

While she sat in her car and waited for the arrival of Rick and Monty, she listened to the news on the radio and heard a fire had burned down several buildings on Fourth St. and Menaul Blvd. That location had a familiar ring. The more she thought about the address, the more she recalled going there. It was Monty Malone's place.

Just at that moment, Monty pulled up in the parking space next to Monica. She rolled down her window and called out, "Did a fire burn down your store?"

"What?"

"I just heard about a fire on Fourth and Menaul. Isn't that close to your business?"

"Yes, that's my address. My God, I still have all my boxes of books in there. I'll call my friend who owns the record store next door." Monica saw Monty punch a number into his cell phone.

Monica got out of her car and stood by her front fender. She didn't want to look pushy by walking over to his car and listening to his conversation. So she just strained her ears and hoped she'd hear at least his end of the exchange.

Monica saw Monty put his phone back in his pocket. His head drooped as he stumbled over to her. "The fire blackened my chairs and charred my books. Everything is unusable." Monty nudged his toe into the gravel and kicked a couple stones.

"Do you have insurance for your property?" Monica doubted he had been that prudent since he seemed to live in a fantasy world most of the time.

"No, I didn't think anything would happen. But now I can't go back to my old life. I've burned my bridges, or my bridges have been burned, so to speak."

He paused a moment and appeared to be in deep thought. His face suddenly brightened. "Maybe fate burned down the building so I could change my life. I'm free of indecision. Lady Luck has smiled on me."

Monica said, "You truly are an optimist." She was surprised he bounced back so quickly.

"Thank God, I took my money tree over to my apartment. It's my favorite thing in the whole world."

"It's a nice money tree. Actually, I've never seen any others, but I'm sure it's beyond compare," said Monica who didn't know what else to say about a plastic money tree.

"I've put examples of all my forged bills on it. My $20 bill is my best one. On the $5 bill I smudged a little of the ink, but you can hardly see it, and the $10 bill has too many lines. A bank would spot it immediately."

"I hope you don't try to pass those $20 bills of yours," cautioned Monica. She had mentioned this before, but she still wasn't convinced he hadn't spent some at high traffic places such as a grocery store, a gas station, or a movie theater.

"Oh, no, I wouldn't do that. I just used the bills for publicity. But since I'm no longer selling books about making money, I use my dollar tree to enhance my apartment, sort of like a potted palm. A little greenery always warms a room. I even bought a book on feng shui so I could put my tree in the right spot." Monty spoke with pride in his voice.

"Feng shui? How does a money tree work into the spiritual harmony of your interior decor?" asked Monica who wondered why anyone would want a plastic tree with phony money in the house at all.

"The living space of your home is very important for inner peace and harmony. I can't just put that tree any place. It has to contribute to the flow of good energy and integrate my ying and yang," explained Monty.

"Where did you put it?"

"Right now, it's next to my brown leather chair which gives the room balance."

"How?" asked Monica who wasn't following his train of thought.

"On one side of my chair is my old life, and on the other is my new life which is a file cabinet full of ideas for my new profession as a pimp. I put a little blue bowl of colored jelly beans with a chia pet on top of the file cabinet for a little color."

"Perhaps a few Christmas ornaments would give your tree a little color, too. By the way, what do you have in your file cabinet?"

"All sorts of things. Since I have to decorate each girl's room, plan the reception area, and furnish my office, I need to be organized. In my file, I have scraps of fabric for the drapes, paint chips for the wall colors, and photographs of furniture."

"You seem to be very concerned about the living conditions of the girls," Monica said.

"I have other plans as well. I want a logo for my stationary which says Monty's Kitties and has a picture of a winking kitten. I'll be like Hugh Hefner with his bunnies. Jack Jones and I are meeting next week to work out the details. He wants me to order fridge magnets which the girls could give to their clients."

"I doubt if the girls or their clients would put them on the doors of their refrigerators. Save your money," advised Monica.

"I'll think it over. I'm going to offer the girls other benefits. If I can rent enough space, I'd like to give the girls small areas of land so they could do a bit of gardening, just a few flowers and maybe a tomato plant or two."

"I doubt if the girls want to garden. Actually, I've never heard of a *ho* that used a hoe." Monica chuckled at her little joke.

"That's not funny. These girls have hobbies just like we do. They're not aliens from another planet." Monty's jaw stuck out, and his voice had an edge.

"Have you ever met one of these ladies of the night? I'd bet their hobbies are heroin, meth, opium, ecstacy, or crack." Monica tried to point out the disadvantages of the pimp profession every chance she got.

Before Monty could reply, Rick arrived. The detective waved and gave Monica a special smile before he greeted Monty. Now the interest in Nick's belongings became everyone's concern. All three of them walked down the line of units until they came to #54. Monty opened the door, and they went inside.

A couple paintings of old adobe houses, a pair of rubber waders, and other odd things, along with several shoe boxes littered the floor. Monty said, "None of those boxes are mine. They must belong to Nick." He prodded a couple boxes with his toe.

Rick zeroed in on a dusty box tucked away in the corner and partially hidden by a baseball and glove. He picked it up and blew away part of the covering of dirt. After lifting the cover, all three peered into the box. There were stacks of $20 bills. "Are you sure these aren't homemade?" asked Monica.

"No, mine are crisp and fresh looking, like they just came off the press," answered Monty.

Rick flipped through the bills and whistled. "Looks to me like a couple thousand."

"Blackmail money. I bet it's blackmail money, or else he would have put it in the bank," said Monica who felt elated on their finding this good clue.

Rick opened another box and found more bills.

Monty said, "I told you before, Nick kept talking about Paris, a new car, stuff like that. I thought he was just blowing hot air." Monty pushed all his things to one side so Rick could easily see what belonged to Nick. He wiped his dusty hands off on his pants.

Monica opened another box which contained money. The fourth box was empty, and the other two had odd trinkets: ash trays from hotels, a couple ballpoint pens, a flashlight , a day planner, several paperback books, and paper clips.

Rick immediately took out the day planner and thumbed through the months. His eyes focused on the pages with full concentration. Monica, of course, knew he had first dibs, but she wished she had pulled it out. She inched closer to him and looked over his shoulder so she could read it too.

While Monica maneuvered to get a peek, Monty took down a Lobo football pennant, dangling from a baseball bat and appeared to be disinterested in the little calendar Rick was reading so intently.

As Rick flipped through the month of Rob's death, Monica skimmed the writing. He had a dental appointment, many dates with restaurant names and times with the letter T written beside them, and one mysterious notation on a Saturday night.

She scrunched her eyes and made out a 12 and a wavy line with loops which could be almost any letter or letters of the alphabet. When Rick opened to a previous month, the same notation on a Saturday night was there.

"Could that be a date and time for a meeting with the person he was blackmailing?" asked Monica. "Or perhaps it's a pick-up time, just like the spies in the movies who go to a certain wall where a message is hidden behind a brick"

Rick answered softly, "Yes, I think it's a link to a blackmail scheme. Too bad this squiggle doesn't look like a letter or a word."

Monica picked up the calendar and turned it upside down. "That didn't help. Maybe it's a coded scribble."

"I'll see if the lab boys can make out anything from these hen scratches. We've found important material here. By the way, Monty, could anyone else get access to this unit? Any more keys?"

"No, when I got the padlock, I only asked for two keys. I gave one to Nick some months ago when he asked about more secure storage for a few valuable items he didn't want stolen. The back of the store wasn't well protected. I told him I had lots of extra space in my storage unit, and I gave him my extra key."

"Was he so cheap he didn't get his own storage unit? He had plenty of money," Monica commented as she kept studying the last entry in the diary.

"No, I wouldn't say he was cheap. Sometimes he'd pay for a round of drinks when we went out for a beer after one of my lectures. He told me he didn't have a lot of stuff, and it would be a waste to rent a big storage unit. I never questioned him further. I liked the guy. I miss him."

Monty set down the Lobo pennant he had been holding and looked at the day planner over Rick's other shoulder.

"Maybe we should show that squiggle to a doctor. In medical school they teach them how to write indecipherable words," bantered Monica. Rick and Monty groaned.

"I know it's an old joke," she answered.

"I'm going to load these boxes into my car. Monty, would you give me a hand?" asked Rick who picked up a couple and headed for the door. Monica didn't offer to help. She wanted to snoop while the men were gone.

As she poked around the other odd stuff, she found a woolen face mask used by skiers. In movies she had seen the bad guys wear them when they wanted to burgle a house or commit a murder. As soon as the men returned to get the other boxes, she held up the black mask and turned to Monty, "Is this yours?"

"No, I've never skied in my life. It must be Nick's," he answered. "Maybe he just threw it in here because he was in a hurry."

"Do you know if he skied?" asked Monica. "I don't see any skis in here."

"He never mentioned it. Once he said he didn't like winter sports because of the cold. He bowled, played baseball, games like that." Monty studied the black ski mask. "Why would he buy something like this?"

Monica answered, "Maybe he was paging through a magazine like *Assassins Esquire* and saw an ad for the mask and couldn't resist buying it. You never know when it might come in handy."

"What? Nick, a killer? No. I could believe he might do a bit of finagling to get a couple bucks, but not kill." Monty defended his dead friend's boundary lines. "I mean those boxes of money could have been gotten by, you know, manipulating a few rules."

"Laws. Not manipulating, but breaking laws," said Rick. "I'm taking the mask with me. Look carefully and tell me if you see any other item that isn't yours," instructed Rick.

Monty snooped around in the corners. He lifted his Monopoly box, shook sand out of an old beach towel, kicked aside his rubber waders, and said, "All this stuff is mine."

Rick picked up the other boxes, and they all left the storage unit. After walking out the door, Monty put the padlock in place. While Monica continued to babble, Rick remained silent. "I think men who buy black ski masks want to hide their identities for an immoral purpose," said Monica, "unless, of course, they ski."

Monty said, "Nick was a nice guy. Maybe he bought it as a gift for a skier friend of his. Maybe his rich aunt died and left him the money."

"Sure," said Monica sarcastically.

When they got to the parking lot, each headed for a different car. Rick waved and said to Monica, "I'll call you later."

Monica waved back. "Let me know what you find out."

She turned to Monty. "Keep in touch. I want to hear what happens with your new business enterprise."

Once in the car, Monica didn't know where to go. She had to be at the theater at 6:00 for the second performance of the opera, but until then she didn't have a planned activity. Maybe she could do some investigating on her own.

16

Monica suddenly came up with a daring idea which tingled in her body like a shot of Jack Daniels. She would get into Nick's condo through an open window or whatever and snoop. If anyone saw her, she'd pretend she was his sister and had lost her key.

Of course, she couldn't tell Leslie or Rick because they would most certainly tell her she shouldn't do it. Stephanie Plum sneaked into other people's houses all the time in pursuit of clues, and so did lots of female sleuths. No problem.

She parked on a side street a block away from his condo so no one would see her little Prius. Walking briskly, she entered the area known as The Adobe Village of Roses.

Most of the condos faced a common garden area where a fountain bubbled, and a few pink rose bushes grew. Smaller sidewalks branched off a big center one so each unit's path was connected to the main one. Each red front door had its number painted in forest green. Monica found Nick's # 123 and walked up the sidewalk to the door.

She turned the knob even though she expected it was locked. It was. After glancing around, she noticed each unit had a patio area in the back surrounded by a high wall. Quickly she stepped to the side of the condo and pushed open the cute little gate leading to Nick's walled-in backyard. She felt more secure behind the wall since nosy tenants' eyes could no longer see her. She walked along the side and turned the corner to the back.

On the back wall of the condo was a small kitchen window and a door. When she peeked into the window, she saw a black granite counter with a stainless steel sink.

She took a few more steps to the back door. As she reached out to try the knob, she realized the door stood open about an inch. She almost squeaked in surprise. Was someone in there?

Curiosity stopped her from running back to her car. Perhaps an important clue just lay there waiting to be discovered. Brazen behavior might work. "Hello, hello, is anyone at home?" she called out in a cheery voice. When she pushed open the door, she made as much noise as possible. "Hello, hello," she repeated.

A blonde girl in distressed jeans with lots of trendy holes and a red Lobo sweat shirt stuck her head out of the bedroom door. Her straight hair hung down over her shoulders. She appeared to Monica to be about twenty. "Who are you?" she called out.

It was time to act and answer the young woman. Monica imagined she was Judy Dench, her favorite actress, as she spoke, "Hi, I'm Monica Johnson, Nick's sister. I just arrived from LA. And who are you?" Monica hoped she appeared confident as she told her big, fat lie.

"I'm Trixie, Nick's girlfriend. It's funny, but he never mentioned he had a sister in LA." Trixie moved into the living room and sat down on an old brown sofa. She twisted a strand of hair in her right hand while she stared at Monica.

"Well, we've had our differences over the years. Such a sad time to meet you, Trixie. I had hoped I would be having a new sister-in-law soon." Monica was impressed with her improvisation ability. Taking that acting class in college proved to be valuable. She sat down on a tweed chair across from Trixie.

"How are you holding up?" Monica tried to act in a sympathetic, sisterly manner.

"I cried for hours, but I'm doing better. We were going to leave for Paris in a week. I have the plane tickets and the reservation for the hotel across the street from the Eiffel Tower." After saying Eiffel Tower, she started to weep. She pulled out a Kleenex and dabbed at her eyes.

"You can still take the trip. Nick would want you to go," Monica said as she hoped to gain Trixie's confidence.

"Do you really think so?" Trixie brightened.

"Yes, you should take the trip, for Nick. He would want you to stay at that hotel and enjoy the view. I'm sure." Monica thought Trixie was going to Paris anyway, so she might as well go with less guilt. Also, she might open up a little if she felt Nick's sister supported her. Monica felt sucking up often got good results.

"Well, if you say it's okay. I don't know if the hotel was paid or not. Where would I find his financial stuff?" asked Trixie who was recovering nicely from her previous bout of weeping.

"Let's look in his desk," suggested Monica who couldn't believe her good luck. Trixie had just given her liberty to search the place. They both opened the top drawer of the scratched old desk with its dark rings from damp glasses or cans of beer.

Monica grabbed and read the bank statements which didn't show any large deposits outside the checks from Monty and the bowling alley. She really didn't expect him to put any of his blackmail money in the bank since he obviously preferred the shoe box method. The current bank statement hadn't arrived yet.

"Maybe you'll find he paid for the hotel when this month's statement comes," said Monica as she kept pawing through the papers.

"You're right. It could be there. I'll come back in a couple of days and check his mail. I don't want to run into his mother, however. She might not approve that I have a key."

"Don't worry about her. She won't care." Monica couldn't believe how easily she fabricated a new persona. She had just given Nick a nice, liberal mother.

While she talked, she kept looking at the bank statements. Nick didn't have much money in either his checking or his savings account and no reference to a safe deposit box. Both women sifted through a pile of old receipts for clothes from Macy's, groceries from Albertson's, and even rental movies from a variety of places.

After rummaging through all the desk drawers, Trixie sat on the floor. "If he didn't pay for the room at the hotel, I don't know if I can go. I'm a student at the U, and I work as a waitress at the Hairy Ape Bar on Central Ave. so I don't have much money to spend."

Monica kept flipping through other pieces of paper while Trixie talked about the planned excursion. The rest of the paper stuff consisted of grocery lists, coupons for restaurant freebies, and an unpaid dentist bill.

Trixie continued, "He said he was going to buy me French perfume and diamond earrings after we got to Paris." Trixie's tears welled up again as she contemplated the loss of expensive jewelry.

"Did he indicate how he was going to get the money for the hotel, the jewelry, and the airline?" asked Monica who went back to sit on the chair since the desk had not produced a single clue.

"Nick said he had a good thing going which could last for months. And once he flashed about four $100 bills. We went out to dinner at a swanky place, and he bought me flowers and silver earrings." Trixie closed her eyes and hugged her knees.

"Did he tell you what the good thing was?"

"No, and I didn't ask. I thought maybe he was gambling or something," answered Trixie. "He was working two jobs and maybe Monty was giving him some hints about making a million."

"Let's check some other places where he might have hidden information about the hotel in Paris," said Monica as she surveyed the room he used as an office. "He has a big filing cabinet. Maybe there's something in there ."

Trixie stood up and pulled out the top drawer. Both of them lifted out file folders and read the contents. Under A, they found his automobile insurance. Under B, he kept papers from Amazon indicating what books he had bought online.

One of the books was *Paris After Dark*. Trixie jumped up and looked on the shelf for a copy of the book. When she found it, she skimmed through the reading material and concentrated on the pictures of the Moulin Rouge and other clubs. "I want to see these places. We've got to find a receipt for the hotel."

As they continued the search, Monica asked Trixie, "Did the police give you a hard time?"

"Not really, I was working that night until 2:00 a.m. so they knew I couldn't have killed him. Before I told them my alibi, they looked at me kind of suspicious like. Why would I kill a person I loved who was taking me to Paris? Honestly, those cops were so lame. That Detective Miller was nice, and besides he's kind of cute."

Monica smiled to herself when she heard the comment about Rick. He really was cute with his hair tumbling off his forehead and his brown eyes twinkling. But she turned back to her goal of investigating a murder. She needed to get Trixie talking. Monica decided to be blunt. "Do you think Nick was blackmailing someone?"

Trixie looked up from her file folder and rested her eyes directly on Monica. "Yes, I wasn't going to say it, but I thought so from the moment he started showing off his money. I didn't know if I should tell you, since you're his sister and all, but there were lots of signs."

"I'm realistic about my brother. He always took shortcuts, even as a child." Monica remembered one of her own naughty shenanigans to use as an example. "Once when it was his turn to wash the dishes, he let the dog lick them. Then he just put them back on the shelf."

Trixie smiled at Monica's anecdote.

"What did he say that made you suspicious he was blackmailing someone?"

"Well, a couple weeks ago we were talking about business, and I said who you know is important. He laughed and said it's *what* you know that's even more important. When I asked him to explain, he just said something about dirt bringing in the money. I asked if he knew some dirt. He laughed again and said he might." Trixie grabbed file folder C while she talked.

"Do you know when he met with his vic–, his business source?" asked Monica.

"I'm not sure, but I think on Saturdays. Sunday really isn't a big date night, but we often went out to a fancy dinner then, and he always tipped generously. Sometimes if we went to the Old Town area to eat, we'd pass by an open jewelry store. If I really admired a necklace in the window, he'd buy it for me. I really miss him."

Trixie's eyes watered a bit, and she used a finger to catch the tears.

"Since he was murdered on a Saturday night, probably the person he was blackmailing killed him. Did he give you any hints if this person was a man or a woman?" Monica doubted if Trixie knew, but she asked anyway.

"No, I have no idea, but he said something weird that could indicate he was blackmailing some-one. Once I asked him where he got all the money to take me to Paris. We were right here in his place. He pointed to the desk and said something silly."

"What did he say?"

"He said the goose was right there, and her golden eggs would just keep on coming. Then he laughed."

After hearing those words, Monica went back to the desk and turned a drawer upside down, pushed a finger into the space where the drawer had been, and felt around for a secret hiding place.

Trixie helped her check under each drawer and under the desk itself. Tapping the sides, pressing along the edges, even shaking the desk didn't reveal a hidden compartment.

"He moved whatever evidence he had," deduced Monica. "It must have been smallish, probably photos or letters. Where do you think he put the stuff?"

Trixie said, "I don't know. Maybe in the water compartment in the toilet, behind a picture, under the lining of a chair. That's where they look in the movies."

"I'm sure the police checked all the obvious places. We need to be creative thinkers," said Monica.

"Why are you so anxious to find this evidence of his blackmail? Were you thinking of taking over and making a little money on the side?" Trixie lifted an eyebrow and cocked her head.

"No, no, I would never do that. It's illegal and immoral. I want to give the evidence to the police," said Monica emphatically.

"I don't think blackmail is so bad. It's punishment for the person who did something wrong. Sort of like vigilante justice. Nick acted like both a policemen who caught a bad person and a judge who gave the bad person a fine."

After Trixie proclaimed her opinion on blackmail as being an honest response to criminal activity, Monica shut her mouth.

"I'd like to see you again. Do you work every night at the club?" Monica asked.

"Just on Fridays and Saturdays. During the day I take classes at the University. Our fall break is next week, and I planned to spend that time in Paris hanging out at the Louvre during the day and the clubs at night." Monica could see tears forming in her eyes again.

"Are you a fine arts major?"

"Yes, I paint."

"I'd like to see your work sometime."

"I paint in the style of Matisse who was just the greatest ever. I've copied all his work so I could get the feel of his strokes and be part of his genius. An artist melds with his painting so the paint is like skin, and the ecstasy of creation is like the uniting of souls." Trixie's skinny arms crossed over her chest, and her eyes closed.

"Does a painting have a soul?" asked Monica who didn't follow Trixie's creation theory.

"Yes, yes, yes," said Trixie who still had her eyes shut.

"I assume you know Monty Malone since Nick worked for him," said Monica who decided to change the subject.

"Oh yes, he's an artist, too. But he prefers com-mercial art. Have you seen his twenties? They're really great. I couldn't find a flaw. You know printing your own money helps the economy," Trixie said in a matter-of-fact voice.

Monica thought Trixie had a unique way of look-ing at felonies. "How does it help the economy if you make your own money?"

"It keeps money flowing. Each transaction is a part of the flow. The more flow, the more people get goods and services. One twenty could give one person a meal, another a shirt, the third a pair of shoes. Every-one benefits," Trixie explained.

Monica felt she had to stand up for law and order. "But forgery is illegal. They put forgers in prison for long periods of time."

"This country needs to loosen up," answered Trixie. "The police are so picky."

Monica agreed, "Yes, the police are picky." After that analysis of the law, Monica decided she couldn't get any more information from Trixie. They both sifted through the rest of the file cabinet which only contained basic, ordinary data.

Trixie returned all the folders to the drawer. She hesitated for a moment and blurted out, "I feel I should tell you I'm not going to the funeral. Since your mother wants the body sent back to Wisconsin, I can't afford to fly there. I'm sorry. I really did love him."

"Mother will understand. Don't worry about it." Monica felt instant relief. She hadn't thought about all the implications of her lies. If Trixie and his mother didn't get together, maybe she wouldn't be found out.

Monica's conscience started to bother her, and she remembered the old adage about lying. Once you lie, you weave a web that leads to more lies. She would have to go home, sip a glass of wine, and figure out a good way to come clean.

"I need to run some errands. It was nice meeting you, and I hope you find evidence that the hotel has been paid." Monica headed for the back door.

"Bye, nice meeting you," responded Trixie who tipped a stuffed chair over to inspect the lining as she spoke.

As Monica pulled away from the curb in her Prius, she reviewed her conversation with Trixie. That girl knows more than what she told me. If she had known about the Honest Abe Storage unit and found the key, she would have cleaned it out. She'd probably justify taking the money by thinking Nick wanted her to have it and spending it would help the economy.

Monica's conscience gave her another tweak about lying to Trixie. At the same time, she smiled and thought it was kind of fun.

17

After her afternoon attempt at investigating, Monica went to the theater for the second performance of the opera.

She noted the atmosphere had changed from the previous night. The high tension, the jitters of the first night, and the expectation of the ghost seemed blunted. Monica could feel the difference as the members of the company talked to each other in subdued voices rather than high pitched nervous tones of the previous performance.

The clarinet player and the drummer, yawning and fiddling with their instruments, sat in the orchestra pit. Hugh chuckled at somebody's joke while a scowling Cap checked his new cameras.

Monica didn't get a bang out of putting on her heavy makeup and fancy wig like she did the night before. While she milled around in her costume, the cast members grumbled about not having any festivity after the performance. Tonight, people would celebrate in small groups or go home to rest.

Rick had invited her to a late supper or late ice cream sundae, whichever she preferred. She looked forward to chatting with him, but they saw each other a lot so the event wouldn't be extra special.

When she saw Cap fussing with a camera lens, she asked, "Any paranormal activity today?"

"Nothing. Quiet night, quiet day."

"Good, or rather too bad, or things could change," stammered Monica as she groped for a supportive answer.

"I stayed here until 3 a.m. One of my boys stayed until dawn. Quiet as a tomb. It's getting harder to find ghosts these days. For years I've been to haunted lighthouses, mausoleums, graveyards, amusement parks, and lots of old houses, but I'm running out of spooks. I'm worried my show could be canceled."

"I never thought about the problem of a scarcity of spooks."

"In my business, it's a calamity. I might have to switch to another type of show. I've been thinking about doing a reality show." Cap stopped fussing with the lens of the camera and stroked his chin where a tiny Van Dyke beard grew.

"What do you have in mind?" Monica hated reality shows and the thought of another seemed a waste of TV time.

"Have you seen the cooking shows where chefs have a time limit to prepare a dish using certain ingredients? Another reality show is framed the same way but with dress designers who have to create an outfit with specific fabrics. I have a terrific idea which follows that plan." Cap's eyes danced as he spoke.

"What is it?"

"Fix the Nerds."

"What do you mean? Are you referring to dorks, people who don't fit into mainstream society?"

"Yes, of course. I'll select five nerds from various high schools across the country and five shrinks. Each shrink will have a month to change his nerd from wearing a pocket protector to wearing sagging jeans."

"The nerds don't wear pocket protectors anymore. That is no longer a signature of nerd wear," said Monica who saw teenagers in various outfits every day.

"What is?"

"It's more complicated. They don't know the current teen fashion. They just look odd." Monica tried to come up with a specific item that identified the nerd.

"I'll have to do some research," admitted Cap. He set his camera lens on the table and looked off into the distance as he thought about the problem.

"What's your format?"

"Each shrink will have a month to change his nerd into a regular kid. I'll begin by filming each nerd in his high school where the bullies hassle him, and the girls ignore him. We'll show him with his unkept hair, fidgety hands, and skittish walk. Maybe I'll include an interview where he talks about his hobbies like polishing old stones, collecting stamps, or making bombs."

"I don't think you can change a person in a month." Monica knew some very nice nerds at school, and she didn't think they'd ever change. Besides, she liked them the way they were.

"The viewers will keep watching to see if the shrinks can do it. Each week I'll film a nerd on his way to becoming normal. Maybe an interest in loud music or wearing a tee shirt with skulls will show he's changing. At the end of the month, at least one of the nerds will sag his jeans, unlace his tennis shoes, and text with misspelled words. He'll be a regular American teenager."

"Who's going to judge?" asked Monica, who thought determining that category could be very squishy.

"Sixteen-year old girls, of course. They can tell in a minute. Those girls can spot a nerd a block away. But we need to have a lengthy process in order to increase the suspense."

"Sixteen-year old girls can be sort of mean," said Monica who overheard teen conversations everyday. "I agree they can label a boy in a couple seconds."

"I'll find some sweethearts."

"You know, of course, they'll giggle and wiggle." Monica thought about the tittering and constant movement of the girls in her classes.

"That will just add to their cuteness. On the last program, I'll show a panel of the girl judges looking like young Miss Americas. I'll switch to another room where the boys are waiting to hear the name of the winner. I'll tell them to act nervous. They could crack their knuckles, smoke cigarettes, or beat time to the loud music plugged in their ears."

"You've thought a lot about this, I can tell," said Monica.

Cap continued, "Maybe I'll ring a gong, and one of the cute girls will bring out an envelope. I'll talk and talk while tapping the envelope. I'll rip it just a little bit and talk some more. The audience will be in the palm of my hand while waiting for the verdict."

"What if the nerds don't change?"

"I'll offer a money prize those shrinks can't resist. They'll be working on them day and night." Cap rubbed his hands together and smiled.

"Do you think you should be messing with their personalities?" Monica hated to see anyone manipulated into becoming a *regular American boy*.

"What's wrong with that? They should be happy as they play their video games, cut class, put pictures on Facebook, compete for the number of followers on Twitter, and try to download porn. They'll be able to even flirt with silly, brainless girls."

Monica shrugged her shoulders. "I'm glad you have a Plan B if things don't work out for you here. Lots of people hope you find a ghost, a pleasant ghost, of course."

"Yeah, I need to get back on the job. Maybe if I could get Llorona to come back, she'd contact that wily spook. Do you have another phone number for her?" Cap sat down on a folding chair and rubbed his eyes.

"I just have one number, but I know where she lives."

"I want to film her again. Right now, I don't have much. I need a hot event, a spectacular sighting." Cap stretched his arms over his head like he had just gotten up.

"I can't believe she's trying to avoid you. The other night, she was bragging about being on your show. If you like, tomorrow I'll give you directions to her house. It's rather hard to find since it's on the edge of the city."

"Thanks, I might take you up on your offer."

Monica had to end her conversation when Hugh called the group together for a brief pep talk before the curtain went up.

As the cast gathered on the stage, Hugh said, "You all were great last night. Let's keep up the energy. We're sold out for all our performances which is a first for this opera company. This *Carmen* is fantastic!"

The cast members clapped and smiled. When the oboe sounded the A, all took their places for the raising of the curtain on Act I.

The show went through without a hitch. The singing and the acting reached the same heights as the night before. The audience loved *Carmen*, and the singers loved the audience.

No phantom of the opera appeared or said a word. Monica heard a person in the chorus say, "I think our spook sat back and enjoyed the music tonight."

Cap wrung his hands a couple times and whined, "I need to fill about 15 minutes for my program. What can I use?" But no one offered any material.

The clarinet player put his instrument in its case and left immediately after the curtain calls. The drummer took a lot of time to pack up and haul out all his stuff, but Monica didn't see any twinkle in his eye to indicate any pending horseplay.

After Monica had changed into jeans and a turtlenecked green sweater, she and Rick went out to eat. "Let's go to the Hairy Ape. They have great hamburgers and sweet potato fries," suggested Rick.

"Sure," said Monica, but she had a moment's hesitation. She wondered if Trixie, who worked at the Ape, would be there tonight. If Trixie saw her, would she ask her something about her dear departed brother? That could be very embarrassing.

When they entered the Hairy Ape, it was crowded as usual with college kids and young professionals.

The decor featured drawings of cartoon apes hanging from vines, posing in provocative ways, and mimicking humans in general. One ape with his finger up his nose had the word Dave scrawled beneath the animal. Other apes had names, mustaches, eye glasses, and large sexual enhancements. Many boisterous beer drinkers enjoyed making these small personal additions to the cartoons.

After the hostess seated them at a small table, they scanned the menus. Monica's hunger meter rose once she smelled grilled onions and chile. "A hamburger with all the trimmings and a cold beer sounds great," she said.

"I like a girl with my taste in food and opera." Rick smiled and patted her hand. After the waitress took their order, they chatted briefly about the night's performance. Rick suddenly asked, "This summer the Santa Fe Opera is doing Puccini's *La Boheme*. Do you want to go?"

"I'd love to. It's one of my favorite operas." The fact that he asked for a date months ahead thrilled her since it meant he definitely liked her. "I've never been able to decide which soprano's arias are my favorites, Musetta's or Mimi's."

"I prefer Mimi's, but all the music is great."

They continued to talk opera until Rick's cell phone rang. He turned his head to speak but indicated to Monica he couldn't hear. "I'll run outside so the connection is better. It won't take long," he said as he stood up and walked towards the door.

While she sipped her beer, she glanced at the other customers. Just a few tables were filled. Slow night. Suddenly Trixie stopped at her table. "Hi, how is Nick's sister doing?"

Monica swallowed. "I have a confession to make."

"You're not Nick's sister."

"How did you know?" Monica hadn't expected that response. She felt a flush in her cheeks which spread to her entire face.

"I guessed right away because Nick talked about his brother and never mentioned a sister. I decided to play along with you for awhile." Trixie had an amused smirk on her face.

"I apologize. I shouldn't have tried to fool you, but I had to give a reason for visiting his place."

"I thought you were after something, but I liked it when you said Nick would want me to go to Paris. It made me feel I wasn't being selfish. But I'd like to know why you made up that whole sister bit." Trixie didn't seem to be really disturbed by Monica's deception.

"I'm trying to help the police by getting information. My date is a detective with the Albuquerque Police Department." Monica felt stating his official status would make her mission more credible.

"You could have just asked me."

"You're right. It was sort of stupid to pretend to be Nick's sister. I guess I just got carried away. I took a theater improvisation class in college, and pretending to be another person was sort of fun," Monica confessed.

Trixie laughed. "I like you. You're kind of crazy, but you're okay."

"Thanks. I'm glad you're not mad at me. I just want to help the police catch the killer." Monica felt relieved Trixie didn't bawl her out, or worse, didn't report her to the police.

"I want my Nicky's killer caught and punished. So, I'll help you out."

"Did you see anything that could be used for blackmail?"

"Nope, not a thing." She had hardly finished speaking when a customer held up an empty beer class and pointed at it. "Back to work." She whirled around and headed for the impatient man and gave a quick wave to Monica.

Rick returned, pocketed his phone, and said to Monica, "Lights are going on and off at the theater. I sent a man over to check it out. I hate to make our evening short, but I'd better eat and run."

"Sure, I understand. Could I go with you when you check out the theater?"

"Yes, Miss Marple, you may come with me."

When they arrived at the theater, a police car was parked in front. Several people, who had left various clubs in the area, stood around gawking. When Rick stepped out of his Honda, he must have looked official since a curious passerby asked, "What's going on?"

"Just a routine check," he answered as he moved towards the stage door.

The passerby didn't look convinced since he didn't move on. Rick didn't encourage more conversation since he kept walking fast. Monica followed him like a loyal dog.

When Cap met them at the door, he said, "I saw a light at the back of the theater where all the props are kept. As I headed that way, the light went out."

"Have you checked your camera in the back?" Rick asked.

"No, not yet."

When a uniformed policeman saw Rick, he walked over to him. "I searched the back area and didn't find a thing. I'll keep looking around and go over the entire theater."

"Good. I'm going with Cap to see if his new camera recorded anything," said Rick. They went back where all the props were stored. Cap found a ladder and leaned it against a wall.

As Monica strained her eyes, she saw a tiny camera almost hidden in the molding of the ceiling. Cap climbed up the ladder, fiddled for a while with the camera mount, and brought it down.

Cap, of course, had hoped for paranormal activity but instead he found an image of a regular human being. It was a picture of a dark figure with a flashlight poking into a box he or she had taken from the top shelf. While the figure peered into the box, one gloved hand flipped over either papers or photos of some sort. Suddenly the figure stopped, doused his flashlight, and ran off.

"We have an intruder. What was he looking for?" Rick spoke aloud to no one in particular.

"Maybe he, or she, was searching for evidence that would link him, or her, to the murder." Monica felt this person was the killer. Unfortunately, nothing in the picture gave a clue to the size or gender since a hoodie top covered the head very effectively. One thing was clear. The figure wasn't a ghost.

"Let's look at that box again," said Rick. "We've gone over all the boxes on these shelves and didn't find anything to do with Rob or Nick. What could this person have wanted?" Rick took down the box, removed the top, and looked in it.

The box was filled with receipts. On the bottom of each a conscientious treasurer wrote the check number, to whom the check was written, and the date of the reimbursement.

Monica picked up one and read it aloud, "One large fern, sold on March 15 at Lowe's, reimbursed to Joe Barney on April 1."

"Looking at each one of these little slips of paper will take hours. Frankly, I'm not interested in the mundane cataloging of receipts, but I'll take this box with me and go over it again," Rick said as he lifted the box.

The uniformed policeman returned. "No sign of a forced entry."

"Security is pretty lax here. Who knows how many people have keys? I though after the murder, they'd tighten up, but they didn't." Rick shook his head at the casual ways of theater people.

Monica said, "The killer must be worried. If the police have gone over all the boxes, the murderer should feel he's safe. Maybe there's still an obscure clue in that box."

She wanted to do the investigating of the box, but it was out of her hands, literally. Maybe she could pry the information out of Rick the next time she saw him, or maybe she needed to do some more snooping herself.

18

On Monday after school, Monica went to the Hairy Ape for a burger and a beer. She was hoping she would be able to talk with Trixie. After she ordered, she saw Trixie almost skipping over to her table.

"Hi Monica, I'm going to Paris," chirped the happy waitress.

"That's great. Where are you staying?"

"At that fancy hotel I told you about before. The one with the view of the Eiffel Tower." Trixie looked like a cat that had just taken down a large turkey.

"I'm glad you found the hotel confirmation. It's paid for, isn't it?" Monica knew she really shouldn't ask that question, but it just slipped out.

"Let's say I managed to put it all together. We're planning on hitting all the galleries and museums during the day and the clubs at night. It's my dream come true."

"I'm glad you found someone to go with you. Who is it?"

"Monty, Nick's old boss. I saw him the other day, and we talked about Nick and the trip. Monty is free right now and working on a new career choice so we decided to go together. He's kind of cute, don't you think?" Trixie fidgeted with the menus in her hand.

"Your ahh— arrangement with Monty happened pretty fast. Are you sure you want to travel with him?" Monica wondered if he was a new boyfriend. Nick hadn't been dead for very long.

"Sure, I've known him for months. Really, Monica, I have no interest in him romantically. We're two friends who want to see Paris."

"Do you know about his new career?" Monica didn't want Trixie to be mislead about what he planned to do.

"You mean the pimp thing. It was just a fleeting idea. He loves art, just as I do. He's going to work in that field." Trixie smiled and appeared to be happy about their common interest in art.

Monica remembered Trixie had admired his $20 dollar bill. Maybe Trixie saw forgery as a subcategory under the general heading of fine art. Trixie didn't interpret law as a system to follow necessarily. The fine points or the broad strokes of legality didn't intrude on her way of viewing the world.

Monica decided not to ask what specific form of art Monty intended to follow since it might be better not to know. "Great. The two of you can enjoy the many art museums in Paris. Have a wonderful trip."

"I will. Whoops, my boss just looked over here so I better go." Trixie scampered off to another table where she whipped out her pad and started to take an order.

When the waitress set her plate down with the juicy burger, Monica was rolling around several ideas in her head. Trixie must have found more of Nick's money, or Monty must be printing hot bills. A terrible idea hit her. Maybe Trixie found the blackmail material and took over Nick's job of squeezing money out of a murderer.

While Monica chewed, she pondered her dilemma. She liked Trixie and didn't want her to share Nick's fate. But what could she do? If she told Rick, what could he do? Sometimes her imagination didn't just wander, it galloped like Secretariat at the race track.

She swallowed the last bite of her burger, licked a smidgen of catsup from her upper lip, and wiped her fingers on the paper napkin. She needed to stop speculating on wrongdoing and concentrate on buying shoes at Dillard's special fall extravaganza sale.

As she left the restaurant, Monica waved at Trixie, who fluttered her fingers in a return gesture. Monica realized she had just enough time to drive to Cottonwood Mall where she'd meet Leslie and buy some cute shoes.

When Monica met her friend at the shoe department, they couldn't even find a vacant chair. "We should have come earlier," whined Leslie. "I hate to try on shoes while standing. I'm always afraid I'll tip over."

"Let's enter the fray," said Monica. With a fast movement, she sliced through a stand of women pawing though the racks. Leslie followed in her wake but stopped after she spied a purple platform shoe. Monica was surprised because usually Leslie wore Birkenstock shoes and not trendy high heels.

Monica plunged ahead until she hit the size 9 rack. Since just right foot shoes were lined up on the four tier rack, a salesclerk had to find the left for you in the back room. Monica picked up a red sandal with a tiny leather bow. Cute. She waved the shoe in the air at a frantic clerk who got the message and headed into the back room.

After the salesclerk returned with the left shoe, Monica balanced on one foot while she slipped off her shoe on the other foot. Then she reversed the process so she could wear both red sandals. As she walked a couple feet to see if the shoes were comfortable, she saw Monty sitting on a corner chair in the men's department.

"Hi, Monty, how are you?" she called out while edging over so they could have a private conversation.

"Hi Monica. I'm great, just great," he said while removing a new shoe and returning it to its box.

"I hear you're going to Paris."

"You must have talked to Trixie. We're going in just a few days." Monty put on his old shoes and tied the laces while he spoke to Monica.

"I hope you've dropped the career you were talking about the other day." Monica felt rather motherly towards Monty and hoped to keep him out of trouble.

"Yeah. Art is calling my name. Trixie and I hit it off, and I now see how important art is in this world."

"Didn't you order some night planners and tee shirts from Jack, the Fridge Magnet King, for your previously planned. . . business?"

"Yeah, I did. They looked great. I paid him for the stuff, and I'll keep it all in my storage unit if I decide to go back to Plan A. In this world things change, and I can adjust." Monty looked pleased about his flexibility in switching careers.

"What branch of art interests you?" Monica really wanted to ask if he had gotten out his press and started printing his great looking twenties again.

"Commercial art. I might even do a little work with Jack. He's a real go-getter." Monty stacked up his three boxes of shoes. "Besides these shoes, I'm buying new clothes for my trip. I don't want to look shoddy in Paris."

"Have a good trip. See you later." As Monty walked over to the cashier, Monica followed him with her eyes. Would he pay for his purchase with twenties? To get a better view, she scooted over a few feet in the red sandals and pretended to test them for comfort.

Peeping between two racks, Monica craned her neck so she could see the cashier's desk. Monty stood there with a fist full of twenties. As she watched, he handed over a wad for his purchase.

Monica hurriedly bumped her way through the shoppers to get back to Leslie. She whispered, "Monty told me he's going into commercial art which means he's printing his own money. I just saw him pass a bunch of twenties."

"You can't do anything about it. Ask Trixie to monitor him. Since he likes her, he might listen to what she says," said Leslie.

"Trixie doesn't see anything wrong with it. She told me the economy needs more money to keep up the flow of goods. She said policemen are too picky, and they need to loosen up."

"Most criminals would agree," said Leslie. "But we can't arrest him, so let's buy our sale shoes and go home." Leslie clutched her purple platform shoes as she spoke.

"You're right. But I'm going to tell Rick anyway. He should know. By the way, I haven't heard from Rick about the mysterious intruder they caught on tape. I'd like to know if they found a piece of evidence."

"He doesn't have to report to you. You're not on the force, Monica." Leslie commented while she walked over to the cashier to pay for her shoes.

"I know, I know. I'm going to pay for my shoes, go home, and grade papers. In a couple nights we'll be back on the stage."

As they were walking out of the shoe department with their packages in hand, they ran into the Graingers. "Hi, Meredith. Hi, Milt. I think everyone in Albuquerque is at Dillard's today." Monica said as she greeted her friends.

"Dillard's always has a good sale." Meredith's eyes strayed to a pair of black sandals while she spoke. Leslie hung back which Monica interpreted as reluctance to get involved in the conversation.

Monica, however, wanted to find out more about the intruder so she decided to pump Milt even though she knew Leslie wanted to leave.

"Have you heard any more about the intruder from the other night?" asked Monica.

"No, I went down to the theater yesterday and talked to Cap," Milt said. He was moaning about filling 15 minutes of his TV program. He told me when he saw a light the other night, he thought it was the ghost. Poor guy, his face drooped down to his shoes when he told me the light came from a flashlight, and the intruder was a mortal."

"What do you think about the situation?"

"Frankly, I'm bored with all the talk. All I care about is the opera. Cap did some filming when I was singing. I hope he uses it on his program."

Meredith moved on to check out some other shoes while Milt gabbed with Monica, and Leslie looked bored.

Monica said, "I have a feeling the boys in the orchestra are going to rig up a return of the spook. Do you think anyone, besides Cassandra, really believes in a ghost who's on a vengeful, evil mission?"

"Cassandra is a drama queen. Because of her name, she likes to make predictions and scare people.

By the way, have you noticed any smoke in the air from that fire out in Jemez Valley? Any kind of smoke is bad for the voice." Milt coughed a tiny bit, brought out a water bottle from his belt, and took a couple swallows.

"We seem to keep putting Nick's murder on a back burner while we talk about the show and the spook. Our first concern should be to find the killer," Monica said.

"Leave it to the police. They haven't found Rob's killer yet, so I don't have much hope," replied Milt as he sipped his water. His eyes strayed to a pair of men's sandals, and Monica felt she'd gotten all the info she could.

Leslie pointed to her watch as she shifted her weight from one foot to another.

"I know, I know. But I have to say a few words to Meredith. I won't be long," Monica said as she rushed over to Meredith who was seated on a bench with several boxes of shoes stacked beside her.

"How are you holding up with all that's going on at the theater?"

Meredith looked up from viewing her right foot clad in the new black sandal. "Okay, but I feel so sorry about Nick."

"I've noticed people are more concerned about the ghost than the death of Nick. Why do you think that is?" asked Monica.

"Nick never mingled much. He stayed in the back fussing with equipment, sawing boards, and nailing scenery. I heard he even slept there some nights if he worked late. He was almost part of the scenery himself," Meredith said.

"I think he found or heard something in regard to Rob's murder."

"What could that be?"

"I think he found out Rob's lover. Was Rob gay?" Monica hoped Meredith would tell her about Rob's sexual preference.

" I assume his lover was a woman. Rob was my brother-in-law, but I never asked him if he was gay. Maybe he was still in the closet." Meredith shrugged her shoulders. "I just don't know."

"Theater people have always been liberal and tolerant. They would never care if he was gay." Monica looked at Leslie who was edging out into the aisle.

Monica said, "I've got to go. If you come up with any ideas about Rob's killer, let me know. See you later." Meredith nodded, waved, and went back to viewing shoes.

After Monica and Leslie walked out of Dillard's, they sat down on the sofa outside the store. Small rest areas with comfy chairs and sofas were sprinkled all over the mall. Monica opened her purse to check on her coupons. Leslie leaned back and shut her eyes.

"No more good deals for today. I can't use my coupons for Macy's until next weekend," said Monica as she shut her purse.

"I'm tired of shopping. I should probably go home and do some cleaning," Leslie said.

Switching her focus from bargains to the murder case, Monica suggested, "An important aspect of this murder is Rob's sexual orientation."

"Are you back to the murder again? I thought buying shoes might get your mind off the subject. Why does it matter if Rob was gay?"

"His lover is the key. I just know it. The motive for his death is connected to his hidden romance. He never revealed the name to anybody but referred to his little bird, whatever that means. After being in New York for years, he suddenly returned home. Why would he want to do a local show here in Albuquerque after theater in the Big Apple?"

"Good question. Who knows? We have no idea who his friends were in the City. You should just give up and let the police handle the case." Leslie stretched her legs and yawned.

"I can't give it up. This mystery gnaws at me. Nick knew Rob in high school, and Trixie dated Nick so it's possible they talked about the case. I'm going to chat with her again." Monica perked up the more she thought about Trixie. "Do you want to go to the Ape tomorrow?"

"No, I have lots of things I need to do. We're back on stage on Friday with an early call so we can have a quick run-through. Wait until next week." Leslie looked at her watch again.

"But Trixie and Monty leave on Monday for Paris. I've got to talk to her before." Monica decided Leslie didn't read enough Nancy Drew books when she was growing up. She never developed the nose for sniffing out a mystery. She'd have to do it by herself.

19

"Did Nick ever talk about Rob?" asked Monica as she sat and chatted with Trixie at the Hairy Ape the next day. Monica had persuaded Trixie to drink a Coke and talk with her during her break.

Trixie took a swallow and shook her head. "Not really. He mentioned he knew him in high school, and they played football together."

"I'm really trying to find out if Rob was gay."

"Football players aren't gay. Why do you want to know? He's been dead for over six months." Trixie stopped sucking her straw and looked at Monica.

"I believe Rob's murder is connected to his secret romance. It would help if we knew if his lover was male or female. Did you find any letters you aren't telling the police about? I promise I won't tell." Monica tried to look like a tight-lipped person who would never spill the beans.

"I might have," said Trixie with a little lilt in her voice.

"Would you let me see them?" Monica spoke quickly with excitement.

"How much are you willing to pay? I'm having a rough time trying to make ends meet while I go to school. I have this part-time job, but I need more money."

"Have you offered these letters to anyone else?"

"Maybe and maybe not," said Trixie in a singsong taunting voice.

"You need to be careful. Nick was murdered probably because he demanded more and more money. If this person has killed twice, he or she, could do it again." Monica felt she needed to warn Trixie of possible danger.

"I'm not going to keep bleeding someone dry. I want one transaction, letters for money. It's not blackmail if you sell an item. For instance, I could sell a necklace or a packet of letters. What's the difference?" Trixie arched an eyebrow.

Monica decided not to answer her question. "Where did you find the letters? We looked all over the desk and file cabinet the other day."

"I found them before you arrived. They were in the desk in a cigar box hidden under the top layer of the cigars. When I picked up the cardboard that separated the two layers, the four letters were underneath."

"Who signed them? This could be very important." Monica hoped she'd get an answer to this very vital question.

"You'll see if you buy them." Trixie smiled sweetly, took another swallow of her Coke, and scampered off.

Monica didn't know what to do. She certainly wasn't going to put out her hard-earned money for a packet of letters that might or might not be a clue to Rob's death. If she told the police, which she had promised not to, Trixie would deny the existence of any letters.

While she contemplated the problem, Monty walked into the restaurant. Trixie saw him and immediately went over to his table. They exchanged some words, but Monica couldn't hear a thing. After a few minutes, Trixie took his order to the kitchen.

Monica decided Monty probably wouldn't tell her anything, but since he was here, she'd give it a shot. She got up and walked over to his table.

"Hi, Monty. How's it going?"

"Hi, Monica, just fine. Did you buy any shoes?"

"I bought a pair of sandals. Do you mind if I sit down?"

"Sure, please, have a seat. I come here often because of Trixie. She's such a wonderful girl. My whole life has changed for the better." Monty folded his hands over his stomach which bulged out a bit from his belt and pouched out his white tee shirt with the words, "Give the Ghost a Choice."

"Are you going to protest tomorrow night with Leroy and his gang?"

"If Trixie can get the night off, we're both going to be there. I bought her a tee shirt when I saw Jack. He's sold quite a few already."

Monica decided to blurt out a question about the blackmail. "Do you know about a packet of letters Nick kept in a cigar box?" She stared at Monty who didn't seem at all embarrassed or surprised. He didn't blink or peek around to see if Trixie were listening.

"Trixie told me. I read them, and they're no big deal. Just a lot of those little marks for hugs and kisses and a repetition of *I Love You*. I could write better love letters. But I'm a writer with one published book to my credit."

"Who wrote the letters? That's very important in trying to find the killer of Rob and Nick." Monica's facial muscles tightened and underneath the table she gripped her hands.

"It doesn't make sense to me. Tweety is the signature."

"Tweety, like Tweety bird in the cartoon?" Monica thought giving your lover the name of a lisping canary wasn't very romantic.

"I don't know. Kind of odd, isn't it?"

"Yes, it's odd. I suppose you know Trixie wants to sell those letters. It could be dangerous. I hope you'll talk some sense into her." After she spoke those words, she thought she had just said those words to a man who wanted to organize a bowling team for prostitutes, for God's sake.

Trixie brought over a Dr. Pepper and a hamburger for Monty. When she set the plate down, she gave Monty's cheek a little pinch and said, "I'll be off work in an hour. See you then."

"Monty told me the letters were written by Tweety. I hope you won't get mad at him because he told me." Monica thought it best if Trixie knew. She waited to see if Trixie would be angry.

"I don't care. I've already sold them. See you later, Monica."

"You've already sold them? But you just told me they were for sale a few minutes ago." Monica couldn't believe what Trixie had just said.

Trixie explained, "My boss told me there was a letter for me. I just read it, and the person said I should leave the letters at a certain place, and I would get $500. I'm going to do it. And I'm not telling you where the drop is or when I'm supposed to do it. So there." After making her childish declaration, Trixie marched off.

Monica knew Trixie wouldn't reveal anything more, so she gathered up her purse and waved good-bye to Monty who appeared untroubled by Trixie's business dealing. He just ate his hamburger and sipped his Dr. Pepper.

The next day Monica headed for the theater after school because she hoped to investigate before everyone arrived.

As she drove, Monica arranged her thoughts about the two murders. Rob was stabbed to death after a show on the stage of the theater. Nick heard or saw the murder. He blackmailed the killer with some sort of damaging evidence for awhile until he, too, was stabbed. She had figured out the game plan but not the name of its originator.

When Monica pulled into the parking lot, Leroy and his fellow protestors paraded back and forth in front of the theater. Some wore tee shirts with the words, "Stop Ghost Abuse." A couple others had shirts with "Give the Ghost a Choice." The people in cars honked as they drove by, and the pedestrians smiled.

Besides selling tee shirts on the sidewalk, Jack had branched out and worked up some linen tea towels with the words, "Albuquerque's Phantom of the Opera." Other towels had a picture of the theater with a smiling ghost sticking his head out of a front window and waving. With his white cowboy hat and white eye mask, the ghost looked like a Western Casper.

Monica admired Jack for whipping out those souvenirs so quickly. As he counted out a stack of bills, Monica noted he had made a chunk of money. In fact, the ghost business profited many people: Hugh, the opera cast, Llorona, Cap, even the city.

Since Monica was early, she didn't think many of the cast or orchestra members would be here yet. However, she expected Hugh, as director, would want to be sure everything was in its place so he probably would come a couple hours before the show.

As she opened the stage door, she heard a meow and saw Pyewacket sniffing around. Llorona, dressed in a black satin gown, was talking to Hugh and Cap.

"How did Pyewacket survive the car ride?" asked Monica when she reached the little group of three.

"She rode in the front seat with a window partially open. She told me the trip wasn't as bad as she expected. I had to buy her a CD of *Finding Nemo*, her favorite movie."

"I didn't know cats liked movies. Mine never look at the TV even when there's a cat food commercial."

"My dear, you just have ordinary cats. Pyewacket is special. As a familiar, she has contacts with the spirit world. We're very close." Llorona flipped her long gray hair back over her shoulders and bent down to fumble in her black tote. She brought out a container of incense and lit it.

"I hope you can draw the phantom out tonight. I need more material for my show," said Cap as he scattered a powdery substance on the stage at The Spot. Monica guessed Cap hoped for footprints. It was a nutty idea, but if you believed a spook could saw furniture, you could believe a spook could make footprints.

Maybe the clarinet player would fake some footprints; however, he had no finesse and would probably make it funny by using big clown shoes. Monica could easily believe the musician might pull a trick like that.

"Pyewacket will find him. She can feel his presence." Llorona spoke with absolute confidence.

Monica, intrigued by this amazing cat, pulled over a folding chair to watch the show as Milt burst through the door. The scarf around his neck floated behind him as he strode in. He walked over to Monica and hissed in her ear, "Why is the creature from the Black Lagoon here?"

"I assume Cap wanted another try at an exorcism."

"All he thinks about is his precious show. He doesn't care about art or the finer things in life. He doesn't realize artists are sensitive people. Our voices can be affected by Black Lagoon creatures or other horrible monsters."

"She never stays long. She always chants a few unintelligible words, creeps around in a circle, and leaves mysteriously. Cap likes to film her because she's so theatrical," Monica said as she tried to be like Hugh and soothe the singer.

Milt huffed a couple times and moved over to the teapot on the hot plate to get some water for his tea. As he dipped his tea bag into his cup, he saw Pyewacket and bellowed out in a loud voice, "How the hell did that stray alley cat get in?"

Llorona glared at him and with a voice that dripped icicles said, "Pyewacket is *not* a stray alley cat. She is my familiar. She speaks to the spirit world and has many powers."

"Well, tell her to keep out of my way. My nerves are on edge."

"I will *not* tell her anything of the sort. She was called here to perform a service for the opera. You've hurt her feelings." Pyewacket's hair stood on end while she hissed loudly.

"See, she's very upset and may need some warm milk to calm her nerves. If she doesn't participate, it's all your fault." Llorona crossed her arms over her chest and scowled at Milt.

Hugh hurried over to his star tenor and purred, "Perhaps, you'd like to go over to the Green Room and lie down on the sofa. I'll turn on the radio to the classical music station so you can listen to some Beethoven or Mozart. I'll make sure Pyewacket doesn't come in."

Milt put his hand over his chest and mumbled, "Yes, maybe a little music." Hugh put his arm around Milt's shoulder and led him to the Green Room.

Cap set his camera down and walked over to Llorona. "Sorry, about that. Singers often get emotional." Cap looked at the cat and apologized, " Pyewacket, I'm sorry what he said about you. You're a fine looking cat."

Llorona bent down and whispered something in the cat's ear. Pyewacket meowed a couple times and scratched her ear.

Monica said, "Pyewacket doesn't look angry or resentful now. She seems to have gotten over the insult."

"She'll do her job; she's a trouper," said Llorona who went back to The Spot and began to do her incantation. The cat sat next to her and appeared to be listening. Suddenly the animal's ears went flat, and she crouched into a springing position.

The air, heavy with incense, almost made Monica sneeze. By twitching her nose, she prevented the outburst. She didn't want to invade Llorona's concentration or disturb Pyewacket who looked like she was going to pounce on a mouse or whatever critter had attracted her attention.

Llorona placed nine candles in a circle at The Spot and lit each one with a long match. After blowing out the match, she took a deep breath. Monica scurried up closer so she could see and hear better.

Llorona slowly stepped in a circle three times around the candles while she said, "'Thrice to thine, and thrice to mine,/ And thrice again, to make up nine./ Peace! The charm's wound up.'" Monica recognized again the witches' speech from *Macbeth* and thought Shakespeare is so much better than all that stupid Latin.

Llorona closed her eyes and stood with her hands dangling. Pyewacket, remaining in her crouched position, stealthily moved across the stage. Monica couldn't figure out what the cat saw.

Hugh came out of the Green Room and joined Cap and Monica as they watched the frozen spectacle of Llorona staring at The Spot while the candles flickered and the incense made smog. "What happened to the cat?" whispered Hugh to Monica.

"I'm not sure, but I think she's in the back of the stage. She seemed to be on the scent of a mouse or some little creature I didn't see. Remember Mitsey went berserk here and found that old mouse nest in the box with the dead roses."

"All I care about is keeping the cat out of the Green Room where Milt is resting and listening to a Beethoven symphony. These singers have such delicate nerves. At least, I won't have to worry about Belinda because she likes Llorona. Do you think Burt will be affected by this new mumbo jumbo?"

Monica put her arm around Hugh. He had been comforting everyone, and now he needed a little comfort himself. "I'm not sure what Burt will do. Let's get a cup of tea and forget about it. Llorona may stop her weird frozen staring at any moment, pick up her stuff, and leave before any of the cast arrives. She stalks out a lot without any explanation."

Monica poured hot water into two cups and put a tea bag in each. They sat down at the table and waited for a proper steep time to pass. Hugh broke the silence. "I heard someone is making little ghost earrings to sell in the souvenir shops. When will it end?"

"It might keep growing. I think the idea of spirits from another world coming to earth is an intriguing idea. Perhaps an enterprising person will design a picture of Albuquerque's Sandia Mountains with a ghost flying over the crest. Sort of like Batman flying over Gotham City. The design could be on cups, tea towels, or playing cards."

Hugh said, "Tell your idea to the magnet person, and he'll be selling them tomorrow."

"Yes, he works fast. He probably is improvising right now with his western vigilante spook. I think people basically want a nice, tame ghost."

Hugh removed the tea bag and put it in the trash. "I played along with the ghost thing in order to get an audience so I'm guilty of promoting the idea. But if my singers become edgy and lose their voices, then I've destroyed what I wanted, a great production of the opera."

"Milt will do fine tonight. After he's had his little snit, he'll be in good voice." Monica believed what she was saying. The principals fussed and fumed about their fragile voices, but once on stage they were pros. Meredith always seemed the least nervous of the four.

"What do you think of Llorona?" asked Hugh as he ripped open a sugar packet and added the sweetener to his tea.

"She doesn't seem to do any harm to people. She's got a good patter, a cute gimmick with her crystal square, and an impressive witch costume. The black cat is a nice touch, too. By the way, did I tell you I was silly enough to ask her if she could locate a pearl necklace I lost. She told me to ask my cat, Bob."

Hugh chuckled. Monica felt he was relaxing a bit now. She continued with an idea dealing with Llorona's mercenary bent. "I don't know what kind of a deal she made with Cap, but if he paid her a couple of hundred bucks extra, she'd say the ghost wants to leave Albuquerque and return to the big city."

Hugh's laugh was even heartier this time. "That's great. I love it. The phantom of the opera wants to go to New York like every star-eyed wanna be. I'd even throw in a few bucks for that spin."

While Hugh joked around, Monica felt a little lighter, too. As she sipped her tea, she forgot about Trixie and her mysterious Tweety bird letters.

Nothing was happening on stage. Llorona stood in a frozen pose, and Cap tapped his toe and twitched his shoulders while he waited for the spirit to come.

Belinda entered from the stage door, saw the tableau, and tiptoed over to Monica and Hugh sitting at the offstage table. "What's going on?" she whispered.

"Llorona wants to talk to the ghost. She brought Pyewacket with her to help her contact the Other World," Monica replied.

"Wonderful. She's such a marvel."

Monica carefully didn't look at Hugh and tried to keep a straight face. Belinda nodded and headed off to the dressing room while she hummed the "Habanera."

Meredith entered next. When she saw Llorona, she rushed over to the table where Monica and Hugh were sitting. She sat down and said, "*She's* back, I see. Has the ghost of Rob spoken again?"

"No," answered Hugh. "Nothing has happened. Pyewacket, the super cat, ran after a mouse, and Llorona is just standing there. Cap paid her money for another seance so he's going to be irritated if she doesn't produce. He keeps grumbling about filling 15 minutes on his program."

"Rob wants revenge. He's going to do something. I just know he is," said Meredith in a trembling voice. "Milt tells me all of this is hogwash, but I'm sure it was Rob's voice that called for vengeance." Meredith twitched her hands in a nervous gesture.

Hugh didn't comment about the authenticity of the voice. He said, "Please sit down and have a cup of tea with us."

Monica hadn't realized Meredith had really believed the spook was Rob who planned on getting even with his murderer. She wanted to hear about Meredith's ideas. "Please, sit down for just a few minutes."

"I haven't time. Have you seen my husband? He wanted to come early to prepare himself mentally for his role. He has a very delicate sensibility, you know." Meredith quickly scanned the stage.

"He's lying on the sofa and listening to Beethoven in the Green Room."

"I'm not going to disturb His Highness. I'll just run back to the dressing room." Meredith massaged her neck while she walked backstage. Monica noted the singers touched their necks a lot. Maybe the light stroke relaxed their throat muscles, or maybe they just liked the soft caress.

When Burt entered, he immediately started flapping his arms. "My God, this smoke is terrible. My voice, my throat, my eyes!" He ran back to the stage door and opened it wide while he continued to fan the air. "I can't sing under these conditions."

Hugh noted the incense had created quite a stuffiness on stage. He approached Llorona whose eyes were closed. Very quietly he picked up the incense container and carried it outside. "Enough is enough. The air on stage has to be clear," he said to no one in particular.

Burt stayed outside and inhaled the fresh air while Hugh dumped the incense in the nearest trash can.

Hugh returned, rooted around backstage, and brought out a fan. After he turned it on, the seer came out of her trance.

Monica expected a big argument, but Llorona didn't say anything. She merely blew out her candles and called out, "Pyewacket, we're going home. Come here." Almost immediately the black cat appeared and walked over to her mistress. The two left without a word or a parting meow. Monica thought Llorona fell into her pattern of flouncing out again.

Cap followed her. He probably wanted to find out if she had gotten any messages from the Other World or if the ghost had departed without any fanfare. Monica wondered how much Cap had shelled out for another of Llorona's spiritual sessions with the famous Pyewacket.

The air cleared quickly, but the door remained open as the troops came in. Since the weather was pleasant, the cast and orchestra members hung around the door while they waited for makeup.

They chatted about the high coast of vet bills, the coming election for governor, and the terrible traffic on the freeway. Nothing about the fortune-teller.

Later, they slipped on their costumes, put on their grease paint, and hummed a few favorite bars from the opera.

The oboe player hit the A, and the orchestra tuned up. The opera began.

20

Again at the end of the opera, the audience gave the singers several standing ovations. The principals loved it when they had to return for extra bows. Both Meredith and Belinda received flowers again which they humbly gathered in their arms. The night was awash with love.

Finally, after the audience had clapped their hands sore, the curtain stayed closed. Joe and a couple members of the cast pushed the scenery backstage as the caterers moved in and set up small tables for the shrimp, sandwiches, and little cakes.

Monica took off her makeup and toga before joining the party on stage. As Monica sipped a glass of red wine, she looked around for Rick who had told her he'd be there for the party. Monica picked up a cracker with a shrimp covered in a red sauce. As she chewed, Trixie and Monty walked over to her.

Monica quickly noticed Trixie was not a happy camper. She pursed her mouth into a scowl, jutted out her chin, and shot fire out her eyes.

"That bastard is a crook!" Trixie declared in a strident voice as soon as she reached Monica.

"Who?" asked Monica.

"The buyer of my letters. Do you know what he did?"

"No, what?"

"He stiffed me! He told me to put the letters in a manilla envelope, address it to myself, and put the envelope on the lamp table in the Green Room before the opera. Because of all the confusion, he said people wouldn't take any notice of me. Since he would be attending the opera, he would exchange the letters for the money during the first part of the party. I could pick the manilla envelope up 30 minutes after the party started."

"What happened?"

"I did just as he said. Before the opera started, I put the letters in the envelope and set it on that little table."

"I went with her," said Monty.

"We stalled around and talked to a few people in the lobby after the opera was over. Later, we walked on stage, ate a few shrimp, drank champagne, and stalled some more before I went into the Green Room. I found the manilla envelope, but it was empty. He is a low life bastard! He took the letters and didn't pay me as he said he would." Trixie put her hands on her hips.

"Imagine that, a dishonest murderer." Monica couldn't keep the sarcasm out of her voice, but Trixie didn't seem to see the humor in the situation.

"I can't believe he just took the letters and didn't pay me a single dime. I'm going to the police." Trixie's voice oozed with righteousness. Monty, standing by her, nodded in agreement.

Monica said, "You keep referring to the person who stole your letters as a man. Does that mean Rob was gay? Or did you just guess?"

Trixie had a funny expression on her face. "I don't know. The note requesting the Tweety letters wasn't signed. I guess I didn't think a woman would be a blackmailer."

Monica wanted to point out Trixie was doing the same thing, but instead she kept quiet. Monica shrugged her shoulders and said, "Rick is supposed to meet me here at the party. When he shows up, you can tell him."

Monty chimed in, "We're leaving for Paris next week. We could sure use the money."

"I should have waited and met him. Then I'd have my money." Trixie peered into the envelope again and shook it.

"Wouldn't it be a little dangerous for you to actually see the murderer?" Monica felt she had to bring in some common sense to this discussion.

"We don't know if this person is the murderer. Tweety was the lover and could be a male or female." Trixie wrinkled her forehead as she tried to piece it together. "I don't know how it worked out, but Nick made some money from this person, so why shouldn't I get a few bucks, too."

"This person probably killed Nick because he or she didn't want to pay any more money to him. How did this person contact you?"

"He left a letter on the cashier's counter at the Ape. I guess he dropped it off when nobody was looking."

"How did you tell him you'd sell the letters?" Monica continued to grill Trixie.

"I didn't. He just assumed I would sell the stuff because he explained how he wanted to do the exchange. I would put the letters in the manilla envelope, and he would take the letters and put in the money."

Monica felt a burst of excitement. The murderer could be in this very theater at this very moment. The stage, the Green Room, the aisles in the audience section were filled with people laughing and talking. All the men wore suits so it would be easy to conceal a few letters in the inner pocket of the jacket. The women all had big purses.

Monica looked at faces. Narrowed, dead looking eyes could give away the evil heart of the murderer. She moved her head around to scrutinize each face, but everyone had ordinary features and looked innocent.

After going through her story, Trixie motioned for a waiter to bring over more champagne. Monty lifted one off the tray and joined her in a cool, bubbly drink.

"Did you keep the note asking for the Tweety letters? This could be very important. The tech guys on the police force can analyze the paper, the print, all sorts of stuff." Monica hoped Trixie hadn't just tossed it in the trash at the restaurant.

"Here it is." Trixie produced a crumpled sheet of paper without a written signature, just the typed words of instruction.

"Great. You should give it to Detective Miller when he comes. It might help him track down the killer."

"We don't know he's the killer. He just wanted to buy the Tweety letters. He didn't say he had murdered anyone."

Monica couldn't believe Trixie was so insistent on making this guy or girl seem normal by just having a little something on the side. "Perhaps this person lied to you in the note. Perhaps this person didn't want you to know about the two murdered people."

Trixie took a moment to think over the situation. "Well, I guess you could be right." While Trixie appeared to be contemplating all the consequences, Monica saw Rick coming through the stage door.

"Hi, I'm over here," shouted Monica over the general din. She waved to get his attention. Finally, he noticed her moving hand and headed over to her.

Monica made the introductions. "Rick, this is Trixie Bell. She has some information on the case."

Trixie stammered out her righteous indignation, but Monica noticed she had lost her steam. "This man said he would pay for something, and he didn't. He stiffed me."

"I need to have more details."

"He sent me a letter saying he would pay me $500 for something. I left it for him, but he didn't leave me the money like he said he would."

"What was it you had?"

Monica became impatient with Trixie's dodging around the important nature of what she had, so she just butted in. "She found letters Nick used to blackmail the murderer of Rob Grainger."

"What!" Rick looked at Trixie with incredulous and penetrating eyes.

As Monica looked at Trixie's face, it appeared that Trixie finally had figured out she had done something wrong herself.

Trixie inhaled and stammered, "Well, I didn't know the letters were important. I just thought this guy didn't want his wife to know about his screwing around."

"I need to talk with you privately," Rick said to Trixie as he steered her to the door.

Monica had hoped to hear the conversation, but this time she couldn't intrude. She turned to Monty who had silently been drinking champagne. "Trixie could get in real trouble by withholding evidence. Didn't you advise her she should tell the police about finding the Tweety letters?"

"Well, no. She got really excited about making a little money. As she explained it, she wasn't blackmailing anyone. A person just offered her money for an item."

"I've heard her theories on blackmail and the benefits of keeping money flowing," said Monica.

"I've had my own problems. Change is hard on a person. After I left my old life of Monty Malone the Money Man, I had my heart on the pimp thing. All of a sudden, I started talking to Trixie. She tells me about the two plane tickets to Paris and this fancy hotel close to the Eiffel Tower. She just knocked me over with her fast patter."

"The bright lights of Paris can have an effect on a person," agreed Monica.

"Now, maybe the trip is off. Do you think they'll put her in the slammer?" he asked.

"I doubt it although she's probably going to have some uncomfortable moments when she explains the situation to the police."

"She's a great artist. I've seen some of her work. She paints frozen desserts like ice cream on a tree stump, Eskimo pies in flower beds, and Popsicles on monkey bars. The paintings mirror her philosophy. The Frigid meeting The Ordinary is like man's Indifference meeting Reality. She's real deep." Monty praised Trixie's depth of insight with pride.

"In the painting of ice cream on a tree stump, is the ice cream in a bowl?" Monica was intrigued with this particular painting although all the cold treats placed in unusual settings had a certain charm.

"No, three scoops are off center and sort of oozing over the edge. Vanilla, strawberry, and chocolate. I didn't ask her if the flavors were significant."

"How did she manage to put Popsicles on on the monkey bars?"

"One is balanced on a bar and the other is falling off. She said something about man has to balance his life."

"I've never seen or heard about The Frigid meeting The Ordinary. Next time I see Trixie, I'll ask her if I can have a look at these paintings."

"She has talent, and I really like her. At first I hated to take Nick's girl away from him, but since he's dead, he probably doesn't care."

"You could check with Llorona and have her discuss the situation with his spirit."

Monty shook his head. "No, when we're together, we talk about family things."

"What do you mean?" Monica snapped her head around and gave Monty a sharp look.

"She's my older sister."

"Good Lord, you're related! I never would have guessed it. Did she always talk to spirits and wear funny dresses?"

"No, she got into the spirit business about ten years ago. We both had lead rather dull lives so we changed and went into show business. She took to it like fleas to a hound dog."

"Did she ever show signs of having The Gift?"

"No, she was a theater major in college but couldn't get a job either on the stage or on TV so she took up accounting. Adding and subtracting bored her. Meanwhile she had been reading a lot of books on witchcraft like the Harry Potter series. So she decided to open her own business."

"You mean the fortune-telling business?"

"She didn't like the term *fortune-teller* because it didn't have class. She wanted to be like the Greek oracle at Delphi."

"She's putting on a good show. The incense is a little heavy for my taste, but her chanting and dress can't be beat. Where did she get Pyewacket?"

"I don't know. I think the cat just wandered in, and Betty Ann, her real name, adopted the cat. Pyewacket really adds a dimension to her act."

While Monty chatted with Monica, he kept looking at the door. Monica guessed he was worried about Trixie.

Suddenly Rick returned to Monica. "I'm taking Trixie down to the station to make her statement."

"How much trouble is she in?" asked Monica.

"She lied," he answered.

Monica liked Trixie and wanted to help her. "But there's a whole gamut of untruth. On one end is omission which is barely a lie. In the middle are white lies. For example, saying your friend doesn't look fat in the red dress. On the extreme end is pants-on-fire. For example, saying, you didn't rob the bank. She just omitted a little information."

Rick chuckled but didn't say he agreed. "I'll call you."

After he left, Monica said to Monty, "We have to find the person who stole the Tweety letters. Once the police have him or her in custody, they'll forget all about Trixie and her little omission of the truth."

Monica, energized by the thought that the murderer could be at the party at this very minute, looked anew at all the people swarming over the stage, the Green Room, and the audience area. Laughter and clinking of glasses filled the air.

Monty said, "Trixie and the Tweety Letters. That could be the name of a book. Maybe I'll write one about her, or I could get a ghost writer. Do you think the opera phantom has any literary abilities?"

"For God's sake, no! Forget about all that fantasy stuff. Let's circulate. If you see someone with small squinty eyes who mentions canaries or drops a packet of letters, tell me. The criminal always betrays himself in all the books I've read."

Monica walked over to a group of strangers laughing at a joke. She stood by them and plunged right in. "Hi, have you heard about the Tweety letters?"

She looked at four blank faces. One of the women said, "Pardon me, what was that?"

"I'm sorry," said Monica, "I heard a joke about Tweety letters. You had to be there." Quickly she left them as they blinked at one another.

As she looked around, she decided she needed to blend into the group before asking questions. At the next group, she smiled and joined in with complimenting the performance. "Yes, the singers were marvelous. Too bad the phantom of the opera hasn't made an appearance. Perhaps he knows about the letters and doesn't want to tell."

One of the group asked, "What letters?"

"The letters Rob sent to his lover, Tweety. Nick used them to blackmail the murderer." Monica wondered if her approach was too overt. As she looked at them, she didn't see any guilty expression or nervous twitches on any of the faces.

"Did you say his lover was called Tweety, like the lisping canary in the cartoon?" one of the men asked.

"Yes, that's what I heard," answered Monica.

"Interesting."

Monica left them and grabbed another glass of champagne. As she wondered what Miss Marple or Jessica Fletcher would do, she glanced at a group near the Green Room.

Monty's voice floated over the others. His approach wasn't subtle. "The killer is here in this theater right now." The sentence hovered over the clink of glasses and the general chatter. The people in all the small groups seemed to have heard it because the talking stopped.

"Is the phantom going to appear?" A screechy voice trembled with either fright or hopeful thrill. Everyone seemed to wait for an answer.

Monica tried to decide which notion was more stimulating, a real live killer at the party or an avenging spook floating around in the air. Maybe both ideas excited the people of Albuquerque whose only source for an adrenaline spike was driving to work on I-40.

Hugh took over and in a joking way said, "No killer, no spook. Sorry, folks."

Giggling broke out and more drinking took place.

Llorona in a full black velvet getup made an unexpected appearance. Her long dress and black velvet cape picked up dust as she walked. The hood covered most of her long gray hair, but a few tresses hung over her chest.

She stopped in the middle of the stage, lifted her jeweled staff high in the air, and shook it. To Monica she looked like crazy King Lear standing in the storm and shaking his fists at the thunder. "Speak!" shouted Llorona to the heavens.

Cap whizzed out from somewhere in the back and started filming the scene. His zoom lens spirted out. Monica guessed he wanted a close up of Llorona's intense expression.

"Speak!" she yelled again.

For a moment Monica had a fanciful idea a dog might jump out and bark.

An eerie voice said, "Vengeance." Monica had heard the same raspy voice before. Again she wondered how it was done.

Since Monty was Llorona's brother, he could have rigged up a device and turned it on at an appropriate time. She scanned the area for Monty and saw him leaning up against a wall with his hands in his pockets. Since all electronic devices were so small these days, he could easily be fingering one at this moment.

Monica didn't see Pyewacket. She thought maybe the cat was communicating with her spirit friends and discussing their ideas on unionizing. More likely, she was lying on the sofa and watching *Finding Nemo.*

Llorona gave her staff another good shake and repeated, "Speak!"

"Vengeance," said the raspy voice again. Monica thought the ghost's repertory lacked imagination. Surely Monty and Betty Ann could come up with some creepy, but not too bloodcurdling, dialogue.

"You'll never escape, never." The voice paused for a moment and repeated, "Never, never." The last two words were drawn out, probably for a macabre effect thought Monica, but at least the phantom added a few new words to his schtick.

Cassandra, who was lined up to get her food, shouted out, "More tragedy is coming!"

Monica thought Little Miss Sunshine never failed to add her grim two bits to any situation.

After hearing these two voices, one supposedly from the World Beyond and the other from the buffet line, the party goers stopped talking. Monica wondered if more bizarre effects would take place.

The crashing sound of a vase falling to the floor made everyone flinch. When the vase broke into pieces, the water spilled over the floor where the flowers lay in disarray.

"What's going on?" asked one of the guests, voicing what everyone there was thinking.

Monica saw out of the corner of her eye what appeared to be a tiny thread dangle from a shelf. While all eyes stared at the mess on the floor, she slipped over to investigate.

She saw a bit of thread caught in a sliver of the wood where the vase had been. Someone had jerked the thread, which had knocked over the vase. Probably this person had reeled it in, but the last little part had caught on the wood sliver and broken. But who?

The person had to be close by to manipulate the thread. Monty was still leaning against the wall fairly close to the shelf. Although he was looking at the broken vase, he didn't have that perplexed how-could-this-happen look.

Suddenly a little cup with coins in it crashed to the floor. The coins made a slightly different sound than the breaking of the vase, but still loud.

While a few people screamed, a third item hit the floor just a few seconds later. A ceramic cup broke and odd pencils, ball point pens, and paper clips scattered among the coins and flowers.

Monica kept her eyes on Monty and resisted the temptation to look on the floor. She saw him quickly reel in a very fine thread. He was fast. He didn't look at what he was doing but kept his eyes on the floor along with everyone else. Good old Monty was helping his big sister.

As Monica watched the crowd, she noticed a certain tension intruding on the party. Along with a few shrieks, some women giggled in a high pitched sound.

A few, still holding little paper plates of food, started towards the stage door. They looked around for a trash can and settled on putting their scrunched up napkins and leftover shrimp tails and cracker crumbs on the floor.

Cap had missed filming the falling of the vase of flowers but had gotten the spillage of the coins and pencils. He hustled around getting different angles of the messes and occasionally turning his camera on the stunned onlookers.

Monica felt a certain elation in discovering Monty's involvement in the fallen objects. She suspected Monty had cleverly installed some sort of voice projector which Cap's crew hadn't found.

The raspy voice moaned, "I'm leaving!" Swoosh sounds. A breeze whirled through the stage and knocked over a couple drinks. Monica felt the wind on her face. Swooshing became louder; a door slammed shut.

Llorona sighed deeply. "The phantom is gone." Her head dropped, and it appeared she might faint. Hugh rushed over and put his arm over her shoulder and led her to a folding chair. The people on stage immediately started chattering about the event. The tension in the air had changed to excitement.

Monica heard voices of the party goers. "I can't wait to tell my brother about this."

"Too bad I didn't have my camera with me."

"Where do you think the phantom will go?"

Monica, impressed with the show, hoped Monty might reveal his involvement in order to get a little ego gratifying praise. She walked over and whispered in his ear, "Hey, Monty, that was great! How did the two of you do it?"

Monty's eyes had a little twinkle, and his lips almost smiled. "I don't know what you're talking about."

"You don't need to reveal anything, but I hope Betty Ann pays you part of the take."

"Too bad Trixie wasn't here," Monty said.

"Yes, she would be very proud of you," said Monica hoping her remark might elicit a confession. She thought probably he was dying to explain how he had done it.

Monty said, "Gotta go." He headed for the door before Monica could say anything more.

While people kept milling about and chattering in juiced-up voices, Monica went to the backstage area to see if she could find any voice projecting device or any evidence of rigging the show. She picked herself around two broken chairs, odd boxes, and the J. C. Sandals sign to get to the farthest back area.

She carried with her a flashlight since the main lights in this area were off. Before she turned it on, she heard the voices of Meredith and Milt. They were whispering, but she could still make out the words.

"Rob wants vengeance. He said so. I'm scared," Meredith's voice sounded hysterical as she sobbed loudly.

"For God's sake, stop it! It was all an act. Rob's dead. That God damn brother of mine is still causing me grief. All my life he did everything better. Rob's so handsome. Rob's such a great football player. Rob's so popular. Rob, Rob, Rob!!"

"But, Milt,"

"And then, to top it off, my God damn brother screwed my wife! He just had to put me down again. He always said I couldn't do anything. But I showed him I could sing. When I was getting the accolades, he couldn't stand it. So he screwed my wife."

"Rob wasn't that way."

"Hah! He despised me, and I despised him. But I had the last laugh." Milt punctuated his statement with a deep throated, mirthless laugh.

Meredith said, "I told the police you were with me all the time that night. But you weren't. I tried not to think about what happened. I didn't want to believe you'd do something like that. But you did, and Rob is coming back to get you and to get me. He said he wanted vengeance."

"Rob is dead! That crazy, old lady rigged up something."

"No, he spoke. It's his voice. She contacted him in the spirit world, and he wants revenge." Meredith's voice was rising in pitch while she choked back big sobs.

"You've got to get control of yourself. We'll slip out the back door while everyone is still drinking and talking. If anyone comes over, I'll say you got scared, and I'm taking you home."

A rustling sound indicated to Monica he was going to move out. She had to get out of there quickly.

Her heart was thumping so hard she hoped they wouldn't hear it.

Milt was the murderer! She never thought an opera singer could be a killer. But his old envy of his brother must have gone over the top when he found out about Rob seducing his wife. Sibling rivalry was a strong motive for murder. Brother killing brother even went back to the biblical story of Cain slaying Abel.

Slowly she lifted each foot and tiptoed back to the lighted area where the noise from the crowd resounded. She had to report her news to Rick, but she needed proof. While her brain went crazy taking in her new discovery of the killer, those around her appeared to be energized and having a wonderful time.

Monica edged into a small group and tried to act like she'd been there for ages. The conversation, of course, focused on the electrifying event.

"Wasn't it exciting to hear the phantom speak!" said a baldheaded man.

Monica replied, "Yes, I was thrilled."

"Do you think the ghost will go back to his grave?" asked a lady in a purple sweater.

"Maybe." Monica wanted to say the ghost might head for the Met, but she felt it might be a tad flippant. She turned her head a bit so she could see if the Graingers were leaving.

Milt had his arm around his wife's shoulders while he lead her to the door. She had wiped her eyes, but she was still breathing rapidly in the aftermath of her meltdown.

Monica wished she had recorded the conversation because both Meredith and Milt would deny the accusation. She wanted to tell Rick immediately, but he was at the station grilling Trixie. At this point she couldn't do anything except make polite conversation with the opera goers.

Of course, she'd tell Leslie as soon as they left the theater. That would be fun since she knew Leslie would want exact words, nuances, and facial expressions. They would speculate about the Grainger marriage, Milt's infidelities, Meredith's affair with Rob, and the dastardly murders.

Leroy, with a sandwich in his hand, zipped over to Monica. Leroy's words tumbled out of his mouth, "I've been looking for you everywhere. When I didn't see you, I thought maybe you had gone home and missed the ghost's appearance. It was wonderful! Where do you think he went? Did he choose to go or did she force him to leave? What do you think?"

Monica decided to give Leroy peace of mind. "I think he went back to New York. Albuquerque's theater is too small for him now he's gotten such good press. He wants to haunt Lincoln Center."

"Really?"

"Yes, remember Llorona never told him to leave. She just asked him to speak. So it was his choice to go. If he wants vengeance, he can come back and do whatever he wants. But now he's headed for the Big Apple." Monica spoke with a straight face.

"That's a relief. I'm sort of tired of protesting. I've got midterms coming up, and I need to study."

"I'm sure the phantom appreciated your help. Go in peace and study for your tests."

The party goers started to leave after the bubbly was drunk and the sandwiches and shrimp eaten. Monica plucked at Leslie's shoulder as they walked out and whispered, "You can't believe what I have to tell you."

21

The next morning Monica invited Leslie over for coffee. After they were settled in blue chintz covered chairs around the kitchen table, Monica dropped the bomb. "Milt Grainger murdered his brother! There always had been sibling rivalry, but when Rob had an affair with Meredith, Milt snapped."

"I can't believe it," said Leslie as she almost spilled her coffee. "He's a fabulous tenor. Opera stars don't murder people even if their wives are unfaithful." She shook her head.

"That's exactly the way I feel. I hardly slept all night." Monica rubbed her eyes as if trying to get them to stay open.

"Are you sure he did it? How did you find out?"

"Last night I overheard Milt and Meredith talking. He told her that he despised his brother, especially when he found out about the affair. She started crying and said the ghost of Rob is coming after them."

"Maybe she'll go to the police and tell," said Leslie.

"I don't think so. She doesn't have the guts."

"Is it possible he might beat the rap? What evidence is against him? Your testimony of overhearing a private conversation won't hold any water with the police."

Monica sipped her coffee and repeated, "We've got to get him." Monica thought about her fictional sleuths: Stephanie Plum, Jessica Fletcher, Miss Marple.

All of them would do something. Monica decided on a plan of action. "Let's set a trap."

"I think you're crazy if you think you can catch Milt into saying anything the police could use as evidence." Leslie stood up and grabbed the coffee pot and poured herself another cup.

"Maybe we can get Meredith to testify he wasn't with her at the time Rob was killed. Although I didn't hear her say it, she could probably make the same statement about the time of Nick's death."

"What about wives testifying against their husbands? Isn't there some sort of rule or law against that?"

"In the episodes of *Law and Order* I've watched, that point didn't come up." Monica picked up her coffee cup and took another sip. "Well, maybe we should go back to catching Milt."

Leslie perked up. "I could wear a wire."

"I want to wear the wire. It was my idea." Monica, unnerved that Leslie wanted to take the lead in this caper, felt she should be the one to have the important role. She almost huffed indignantly at the brazen request.

"Yes, but he won't suspect me since I didn't overhear any conversation."

"He doesn't know I heard his conversation. I should wear the wire. I'm more experienced in detection." Monica felt she had to boast a bit to back her claim to the wire.

"How are you more experienced? We both teach English Lit. at Four Hills High School."

"I've read every single Agatha Christie, every Janet Evanovitch, every. . ."

"Reading mysteries doesn't count. They're fiction. You, of course, know what fiction means." Leslie crossed her arms and rolled her eyes.

"I get a lot of information from those books. But why are we arguing anyway? We can both wear wires. We can switch places and still hear what that smug bastard says." Monica took a sip of her hot coffee after offering up a compromise.

"Well, okay," agreed Leslie.

"Where do we get a wire?" asked Monica.

"I don't know. Where do the characters in your mysteries get theirs?"

"The police keep them in the back room, I guess. But the police aren't going to let us borrow theirs. We could buy them, but I don't know any stores where they sell such stuff." Monica began to get discouraged.

"I'm not going to spend my money to buy one. I guess the wire issue is a lost cause," Leslie said as she poured more coffee into her cup.

Monica nodded. "Let's consider how we can maneuver either one of them to talk." Monica knew getting one of them to spill the beans was another sore spot in their plan.

"How can we do that?"

"Force and trickery, two of the basic ways, involve brawn or smarts. Brawn is out of the question so we'll have to rely on our creativity to compose a false story to finagle a confession."

"Forget it. We should let the police pursue the investigation. By the way, did you tell your detective friend about Milt's confession?" Leslie's voice showed signs of loss of gumption.

"Yes, I told Rick. He didn't seem real surprised so he might know something that he didn't tell me. But I still want to be in the game. I can do things the police can't. The theater class I took in college helped me the other day when I pretended to be Nick's sister. Maybe I'll just use that skill again." Monica's eyes gleamed as she thought about the joy of playing a scene.

"How are you going to get evidence of the confession, if there is one?"

"I'll plant my old class recorder in a room," answered Monica confidently.

"And where is this room?"

"I'll have to work it out." Monica realized there were tiny flaws in her fancy plan.

"Monica, do you realize your play-it-by-ear scheme has a 1% chance of working?" Leslie shook her head to emphasize the futility of this harebrained idea.

"Wait and see." Monica took out some Oreo cookies from the shelf and put them on the table. Both she and Leslie grabbed one and chomped away while they thought about the dilemma.

Monica burst out with an idea. "The Green Room is a good place for the recorder. I can put it on the shelf with all the books and other stuff so it won't be seen. There are two big easy chairs by that shelf and a little table close by. I'll get Meredith to sit in one of those chairs. It's a perfect trap."

"And how are you going to get Meredith to go to that room, sit in that chair, and spill her guts?" Leslie yawned and swirled her coffee before taking another sip.

Monica gave Leslie a mysterious smile. "I'll need the help of our beloved seer." As she formulated her conversation with Betty Ann better known as Llorona, she leaned down and scratched behind Mitsey's ears.

The dog stopped sniffing for fallen crumbs and sat still with a look of ecstasy on her face.

Excited by her creativity, Monica punched in Betty Ann's number. "Hi, this is Monica Walters. I need some help in getting evidence against the person who killed Rob."

"I know who did it. Milt Grainger. Pyewacket already fingered him." Llorona's voice was matter-of-fact. "That should be enough evidence."

"Pardon me. What do you mean Pyewacket fingered him?" Monica couldn't believe her ears. She thought she'd have to convince the woman Milt had murdered two people by recounting the conversation she overheard.

"Don't you remember Pyewacket hissed at Milt. I covered it up by saying she was insulted by his calling her an ordinary stray cat. In reality, the spirit of Rob pointed out his murderer to Pyewacket. I told that nice young detective afterwards. I, of course, don't know what he did with the information. The police, you know, are so picky about their evidence."

"Yes, they are. That's the reason I want to record Milt's wife saying he wasn't home with her the two nights of the murders. Could you help me by urging her to go the theater's Green Room tonight at 7:00? You could say Rob's spirit wants to talk to her."

"Yes, I will. I don't like that Milt person. Besides killing people, he's a bad singer. He was flat all night in his last performance. I couldn't understand why the audience stood up for him. The opera world would be better off without him. I'll do it free of charge."

"Great. I'll have everything set up beforehand." Not only was Monica relieved Betty Ann had agreed so quickly but that she wasn't charging her.

"I'll summon Rob's spirit. He took off in a huff, but he'll come back because he has a real strong need for revenge. By the way, Rob was really touched by that college kid, Leroy. He was grateful for his sensitivity to his mental health when he picketed the theater with his 'Stop Ghost Abuse' sign."

"Next time I see Leroy, I'll tell him. Knowing he helped a needy ghost will make him feel good."

"So many people don't care about the spirits. They just forget about them and their needs." Betty Ann seemed very pleased about Leroy's efforts.

"Will Pyewacket want to come?" Monica thought the cat might enjoy the scene.

"Pyewacket may not want to come. She feels she's already done her duty. And I don't insist since I've heard all this union talk."

"See you then." After Monica ended the conversation, she helped herself to another Oreo and another cup of coffee. She needed to locate her recorder she used for her classes, set it up in the Green Room, and convince Leslie to go with her to the theater. She knew Leslie responded to treats just like Mitsey so she used a good enticement.

"If you go with me tonight, I'll buy you a hot fudge sundae."

Leslie didn't hesitate. "Okay. But don't drag out the conversation with Meredith. I have a lot of papers to grade."

That evening Monica and Leslie waited in the car for the other participants. Earlier in the afternoon, Monica had placed the recorder on the shelf and hidden it behind a vase of paper flowers in the Green Room.

The oracle's car and Meredith's station wagon arrived simultaneously. All four people got out of their cars and walked to the stage door.

Clad in her traditional black gown, Llorona announced to the other three, "The spirit of Rob has requested this meeting with Meredith. Monica, you and Leslie may stay to make her more comfortable, but Rob may ask for privacy."

Monica and Leslie both said almost in unison, "That's fine."

Meredith appeared to be a bit shaky. "I'm really nervous. I don't know if I should be here or not. Milt had to meet with a client so he doesn't know I'm doing this. He wouldn't approve, I know." Meredith sidled over to be closer to Monica, rather than Llorona who did make rather an imposing figure.

Monica used Hugh's key to open the door. She heard Meredith swallow and hang back. In order to reassure the timid Meredith, Monica said, "Don't worry. It'll be fine."

The group turned left and went towards the Green Room. Monica reached the door first. She opened it, glanced in, and shut the door immediately. "Milt's *doing it*! I don't know who the woman is because she's underneath. . . but they're *doing it*. I've never seen anyone *do it* before. Yuk!" squealed Monica as she shut her eyes. "Don't look in there. It's icky!"

"What?" three voices said together as three hands reached for the door knob.

Leslie, the first to grab the door knob, opened the door wide. Monica closed her eyes, but the others looked in.

"Awful!" Leslie said and slammed the door. "I've never seen anyone *do it* before either. I'd like to erase my eyeballs."

Meredith on the other hand screamed, "Milt! You bastard!" She flung the door open, stormed in with blood in her eye, and jerked the hair on the back of Milt's head. In her fury she yanked his hair so hard that his neck bobbled like a rag doll.

Immediately, he tried to reach around and grab her hand to stop the abuse, but her grip was strong. Finally he managed to jerk his way out of her reach while getting off his lover.

The two people who had been *doing it*, scrambled around to cover their naked parts while Monica covered her eyes with her hand. But a few seconds later, Monica couldn't resist peeking through her fingers to watch the goings-on.

Shaking with anger, Meredith tried to kick Milt while he danced around on one foot as he tried to get his pants on. She kept repeating, "How could you do this, you bastard! You promised me over and over you had stopped screwing around with every skirt you saw. You promised me!"

With a powerful swing, she managed to give him a good kick in the groin. He bent over in agony, got tangled in one of the legs of the pants, and fell over.

"I can explain. I can explain, " he yelled as he rolled around with his hand on his crotch. He tried to stand up and pull on his pants at the same time. "This isn't what it looks like."

"Of course it is!" she shrieked while she tried to kick him again as he dodged around in awkward positions. Monica thought he looked like a giant crab as he made funny little movements to get away from Meredith's pointy-toed shoe.

While Meredith focused her wrath on her errant husband, Belinda backed away out of reach of the hysterical wife and tried to put on her skirt. She grabbed her blouse, and said to no one in particular, "Sorry, about all this. Tenors are so emotional, so passionate. I was married to three of them."

Her words made Meredith turn around and focus on the offending woman. "And you!" squawked Meredith, " should know better, you bitch!"

"Darling, you're so right. I never should have let my baser instincts take over. But in the opera we were lovers, and it just spilled over." Belinda shrugged her shoulders. In her haste to cover up, she hadn't buttoned her blouse correctly so it hung unevenly over her skirt. She didn't stop to fix it but hurriedly looked around for the rest of her clothes.

Monica thought it probably was wise for Belinda to make a hasty retreat. During all of this commotion, Llorona stood in the corner and remained silent.

While Meredith switched her ire to Belinda, Milt frantically tried to gain his balance and get a leg into his pants. Monica put her hand down from her eyes so she could follow the action better. Her head swivelled back and forth from one person to another.

Puffing heavily from her exertion, Meredith stopped to catch her breath. During this moment of silence, Belinda grabbed her purse in one hand and her shoes in another. She ran like the devil was at her heels and made her escape.

After Belinda left, Monica felt it was time to ask questions. Meredith's fury might goad her to blurt out the truth. Quickly Monica butted in and asked, "Was Milt home all night when Rob was killed?"

"No, he wasn't. I covered for him, but he was gone a couple of hours. I'll change my statement I made to the police." Meredith had a triumphant tone to her voice. She continued, "Thousands of dollars have been taken out of our savings account which he says went to cover increased insurance costs."

Monica pressed on, "What about the night Nick was killed? Was Milt at home all night?" She hoped the voice activated recorder worked.

"No, he said he met with a client."

"Sweetheart, you're excited. You're not thinking straight. I was home with you both those nights. You got your dates confused." Milt now fully dressed, whipped out a comb and raked it through his mussed up hair.

Monica thought that Milt had his priorities. Even in the midst of an important accusation, he wanted to look good.

"You liar! I want a divorce! I'm going to testify against you. And you sang flat last night!" Meredith belted out her verbal blows. "Flat, flat, flat!"

"I was *not* flat! The orchestra hadn't been tuned properly."

Just when Monica thought nothing else could possibly happen, an eerie laugh came from somewhere. Monica swivelled her head around but didn't see another person. The mirthless cackle made even the feuding couple stop their brawling. Another raspy laugh filled the air.

Llorona pronounced, "The ghost is here. He's having the last laugh."

"It's Rob. I knew it all the time. Please forgive me," Meredith pleaded as she looked up at the ceiling. Monica thought Meredith must be imagining Rob to be hovering in the air above them on some invisible indoor cloud.

Right on cue, Rick Miller and two uniformed policemen tramped in. Rick read Milt his Miranda rights while Meredith clapped with glee.

Milt shrieked,"I'm innocent," while they put his hands behind his back and cuffed him .

"That's what they all say," answered Rick in a mild voice.

"I have another performance next weekend. I'll be out by that time, won't I?" Milt looked at all three of the policemen who didn't respond.

Monica turned to Meredith, "What will they do about the lead tenor role? It would be sad if the company had to cancel the show."

"There's a young tenor in voice performance at the University who I've heard is marvelous. He only has a week to prepare, but he's sung some of the arias as part of the opera workshop and with a good coach, he'll do great." Meredith's voice had a lilt of comeuppance.

"What?" shouted Milt as they pushed him along. "No one can replace me."

"You are so wrong," said Meredith. She turned to Llorona and said, "Rob's spirit heard all of this. Maybe he's at peace now. I loved him. He was a much better person than Milt. I should never have married that damn bastard!"

Llorona nodded her head. "Rob tells me he's going to New York. The theaters at Lincoln Center are much bigger and have the best productions. He'll enjoy himself there."

Rick touched Monica on the shoulder as he followed the cuffed suspect. "I'll see you tomorrow night."

Meredith, still filled with adrenaline, picked up her cell phone and punched in the number of her attorney friend. "I'm filing for a divorce tomorrow," she announced to the few who remained.

Monica took this opportunity to ask Llorona, "How did you do the voice and the laugh?"

"My dear, Rob's spirit did the speaking. I had nothing to do with it."

"But when I spoke with your brother, he said you didn't have The Gift, but you had good acting skills."

"Oh, don't listen to him. He doesn't like to think I have The Gift because he doesn't have it. Sibling rivalry, you know." Llorona seemed unconcerned about what Monty said about her. "I hope my brother gets married and settles down. I like this Trixie person. Her name sounds like Tinker Bell. She might have fairy blood which could enrich the line if they have children.

"I didn't know you've already met her."

"Yes, Monty and Trixie came over for dinner. Sweet girl, but her paintings are something else. And all that nonsense about The Frigid meeting The Ordinary. It's a child's dream to find a Popsicle in every flower bed. Trixie does have a charming childish quality."

"I hope Monty finds a new job since he's given up on selling his money book," Monica said. "I like Monty although he's not very sensible."

"He has no common sense whatsoever. I hope he'll forget about that awful dream he had of being a pimp. I think he romanticized the position. He wanted to be like Fred Astaire dancing with all the chorus girls in pink feathers. He loved those old movies."

"I agree he should find a better job."

Betty Ann continued, "I told him he wouldn't be able to go to the 'Rah Rah Albuquerque' festival that the Chamber of Commerce puts on during the summer if he chooses that path. The Chamber doesn't take pimps as members. Monty loves the festival and would miss going to it."

"Getting back to the ghost business. I saw Monty pull a thread to knock over the vase of flowers and the other stuff. What about the voice and the other stuff? How did you work it?"

"My dear, my dear. We might have rigged up a few little bits, but as I've said before, the voice was Rob's spirit. And now I must go. I'll tell Pyewacket all about catching the murderer. She'll enjoy all the details." Betty Ann smiled and walked to the stage door.

Belinda had scooted out quickly before the police arrived so just the two teachers were left in the theater. Monica turned off the lights and locked the door.

She was glad the murderer had been caught, but she hated the idea that an opera singer could do such a thing. Opera singers should devote themselves to art and shouldn't be even thinking of sibling rivalry like other ordinary humans.

The next evening, Rick came over to have dinner with her. As the two munched warm garlic bread and lasagna, Rick added more details about the case. "Trixie kept out a letter from Tweety. She also had a photo of Rob with Meredith. When I talked with her, she gave up the items."

"I was glad the interview with Meredith went so well. Can you use the recording in a court of law?" asked Monica as she sipped her merlot.

"I'm not sure, but I have a written statement from Meredith saying he wasn't with her on those two evenings. We're checking Milt's fingerprints with those found on the knife. He didn't wipe them off very well."

"Do you thing he'll sing?"

Rick guffawed loudly. "Sing? He's singing night and day. He's been running through his entire opera repertoire at full voice and driving the other prisoners and the guards crazy. Also, he keeps asking us if we have a cell with a piano."

Monica recalled that Milt had gone over his arias all the time during breaks in the opera rehearsals. "How long will he be in jail?"

"He'll stay in our local jail until his trial. Since his bail is a million dollars, I doubt if anyone will cough up the money although the guards tell me they'd like to get a kitty together to get him out. They said if his trial isn't soon, they might kill him beforehand."

"Is there anything you can do to stop him from singing?" asked Monica.

"My solution to the problem didn't go over very well. I told the guards to work up a little barbershop music with the guy." Rick smiled as he recalled the scene.

Monica had another question. "What will happen to the money you found?"

"Monty says it belongs to Trixie, but Meredith says it's hers. I imagine the lawyers will get most of it." Rick pulled his chair away from the table and patted his stomach. "Good dinner, Monica."

"Thank you, I enjoy cooking."

While Monica scraped her plate into the garbage, she heard a funny sound. Bob and Marilyn were rolling something around under the table. When she poked her head down, she saw her pearl necklace. The cats were sliding it back and forth to each other. Monica interrupted their game and picked it up. "I haven't seen this necklace for months. I thought I had lost it forever."

"Where do you think it was?"

"I don't know. But remember Llorona told me to ask Bob. I did, even though I knew it was a crazy idea." Monica wrinkled her forehead as she mused about it all.

"We haven't found any electronic device that could have made the voice or the laugh," said Rick. Monica noticed Rick had a contemplative look on his face as if he were trying to figure out this puzzle.

Monica said, "It couldn't be that she really is able to. . .?" As this thought grew in her mind, she quickly looked at Rick for an answer.

"No, of course not. There must be a logical explanation," Rick said.

Mitsey wandered over to Rick and put her chin on his leg. He automatically scratched her behind the ear while Monica hooked the clasp on the pearls behind her neck. Bob jumped on Rick's lap so he had to use his other hand to scratch behind his ears. Marilyn washed her face.

Monica said, "We'll never know, for sure."

Rick replied, "Maybe not, but we have a caged, singing murderer."

At that point, Rick dumped Bob on the floor and gave Monica a long satisfying kiss.